"All you want to do is make trouble!"

"And why should I want to do that?" Drew inquired very evenly, holding Jenna's angry eyes in a long stare.

"To pay me back, why else?" Jenna muttered harshly.

There was the slightest pause before Drew snorted with laughter. "If you mean what I think you mean, then you're mistaken. I have not been carrying a grudge against an eighteen-year-old kid who was too conditioned by her snob of a grandmother to run off with the local grocer's son."

Jenna felt the blood leave her face at Drew's awful accusation. "But it wasn't like that! It wasn't!" she burst out passionately.

Drew looked down at her, his face a mask of emotion that frightened her. "Wasn't it, Jenna?" he challenged, the bitterness sharp in his voice.

Edwina Shore spent thirteen years working in Australia's publishing community, editing mainly academic work, with a few brief forays into general trade or "bestseller" publishing. Now, when she isn't immersed in her own writing, she tries to work in her other interests, which include travel to Great Britain, Europe and throughout Australia, learning Scottish Gaelic, sculpting and painting. She is single and lives in Victoria.

Books by Edwina Shore

Storm Clouds Gathering

Edwina Shore

Harlequin Books

TORONTO • NEW YORK • LONDON
AMSTERDAM • PARIS • SYDNEY • HAMBURG
STOCKHOLM • ATHENS • TOKYO • MILAN

Original hardcover edition published in 1988
by Mills & Boon Limited

ISBN 0-373-02962-4

Harlequin Romance first edition February 1989

CHAPTER ONE

'HAVE you heard Drew Merrick is back on the island?' asked Mrs McPherson at the fruit shop as she handed Jenna her change and watched her face with gimlet-eyed interest that didn't match the airy casualness of the voice.

The question knocked the wind out of Jenna—visibly, if the satisfied gleam in the shopkeeper's eyes was any indication. Jenna hurriedly dropped her own eyes to her purse, her fingers fumbling over the clasp. 'Oh, really?' she said woodenly, which was as close as she could manage to sounding indifferent. She couldn't get out of the shop quickly enough.

The same question was guilelessly tossed at her in practically every shop Jenna went into—the butcher's, coffee-supplier, cake shop; everyone, it seemed, was determined she should hear of Drew Merrick's return. However, better prepared after Mrs McPherson's bombshell, Jenna was able to present a bland expression and say the 'Oh, really?' with commendable lack of interest, defying any of them to guess how her heart gave a sickening lurch at every mention of Drew's name.

Her last call was at the chemist to pick up a prescription for her sister-in-law. There, at least, there was no mention of Drew Merrick, but that was only because the chemist was new to the island and wasn't yet up in local gossip. He nattered on about the approaching storm instead. Jenna couldn't win; she was possibly more frightened of storms than of running into Drew Merrick around the next corner.

The clouds had been gathering rapidly when she left the house, and had thickened and darkened by the time she reached the shopping-centre. Now, as Jenna emerged from the arcade into the car park behind the main street, the sky was a low black roof over the tiny township. Reason, and a lifetime on the island, told her the storm was hours away yet, but the idiotic, childish panic was already taking hold. Jenna threw the bags and packages into the car and hurled herself into the driver's seat as frantically as if the skies had just burst open. And then, when the car wouldn't start, she though she would scream. The battery was dead. Again. She sat there for a moment, forcing herself to take some slow, deep breaths, then, releasing the bonnet catch, got out of the car, raised the bonnet up on its prop and looked desperately around the car park.

Luck was with her in the form of Johnny Adams, the butcher's son, pulling into the car park in his delivery van. Jenna didn't even need to hail him; he spotted the raised bonnet and headed over, manouevring his small van to pull up front-to-front with her car, and when he hopped out he already had the jump-leads in his hand and raised them at her in a sort of mock salute.

'Died on you again, has it?' he grinned. 'Ever thought of putting in a new battery? We can't do a

Lazarus job on it for ever you know, Jenn.' Johnny chuckled at his own corny joke as he yanked up the bonnet of his van.

Jenna produced a feeble smile and slid in behind the wheel of her car without being told, too familiar with the whole routine to need instruction. It was the second time in a month that Johnny had come to her rescue, but he was not the only one; there had been other obliging Samaritans, not to mention her brother, Chris, who sometimes had to get her started at the house. Only it wasn't just the battery that needed replacing; it was the entire car. However, since she'd have been hard pressed finding the money to buy herself a bicycle, all Jenna could do was pray the battered little rust-bucket would hang together for a bit longer.

Battery recharged, Jenna kept the engine revving at a roar while Johnny unplugged the leads, slammed both bonnets shut and sauntered over to her window with the air of someone about to pass the time of day and having a lot of time to do it in.

'Thanks awfully, Johnny,' Jenna got in quickly. 'I'm afraid I'm in a tearing hurry, so I can't stop to talk. Clare is waiting on a prescription, and there's the cooking to get started.'

'Oh yeah . . . yeah. How's business?'

It was a question Jenna hated, but she had unwittingly given him the cue. Business was grim. 'Fine,' she lied brightly, then glanced nervously at the sky.

Following her glance, Johnny studied the ominous sky with satisfaction. 'Storm coming,' he pronounced the obvious with relish.

'Yes.' Jenna bit into her lip. 'Thanks again, Johnny.' She let the engine give an extra-loud roar, hoping Johnny would take the hint.

'No trouble,' he assured her laconically, with a smile that seemed to say it was one of his greatest pleasures to charge up her battery—and, given the monotony of his day, it quite possibly was. 'Did you hear that Drew Merrick was back?' he asked suddenly, bending his long, thin body almost double to peer in the window at her.

Jenna gave a hurried nod and muttered, 'Your dad mentioned it.' Along with everybody else she had come across that afternoon. Except the chemist, of course. She left the township under its black canopy and headed up the main road into the even blacker hills. The island was all hills; hills and pines and steep winding roads that would be the death of her little car yet.

Jenna urged it over the next hill and then saw the four or five cows spread over the road; the last straw. Almost reduced to tears of frustration, she slammed on the brake, rammed the horn and shouted ineffectually at the wretched animals above the din, all the while cursing the island's quaint law that gave herds the run of the island and its roads. The tourists loved it, and no one was supposed to be in a hurry on the island, anyway. Another quaint myth fosterd for the tourists' benefit so that they could go home and tell everybody about the slow, gentle pace of the locals! Not this local. Jenna's hands were shaking with frenzied impatience as she gripped the steering-wheel, waiting for the last tardy animal to move enough out of the way for her to hurtle past.

Clear of the herd, she skimmed down the hill and shot up the next one on the momentum of the gathered speed and a feverish prayer, the dark pines a blur, until she slowed down at last to take the sharp turn to the left which led steeply down to the sea. About two-thirds of the way down, a large area was cleared of pines and, on it, the old, rambling, sand-stone house gleamed an eerie yellow in the shaft of distorted light breaking through a gap in the overhead blackness. Jenna gave an audible sigh of relief as she sped down the slope. Home. Safe.

She turned into the flower-bordered drive, grimacing as she always did as she passed the amateurishly carved board proclaiming 'Grandma's Kitchen' in a swirl of curlicues and garlands. A stupid name for a restaurant. Clare's choice and Clare's artistic handiwork, both wrong, but Jenna hadn't been assertive enough to reject either. She drove up the side of the house, turned the car around so that it faced down the slope of the drive, and parked a little way from the entrance to the kitchen.

Clare was standing in the doorway. 'Here, let me help.' She moved forward, reaching for some of the parcels Jenna was taking out of the car.

Jenna shook her head. 'It's OK, I can manage,' she muttered, managing to gather everything up into her arms to save a second trip.

Clare held the door open, then followed her into the kitchen. 'What's up? I heard you screeching down the hill and I . . . Did you remember my prescription?' She switched the question abruptly.

'Yes, of course I did,' Jenna replied with a snap. 'Sorry I took so long. Everybody seemed to be doing their shopping this afternoon. And then the wretched car wouldn't start. The battery again,' she elaborated, making an effort to take the edge out of her voice. It wasn't her sister-in-law's fault her nerves were at breaking-point. Fishing out the chemist's packet first, Jenna gave it to Clare, then began to take out the rest of the purchases and put them away.

Clare eased herself heavily into a chair and watched her. 'What's that?' she asked with a slight sharpness as Jenna drew out a cardboard box with a local pâtisserie's name all over it.

'Cake for pudding. It'll save us the trouble of making something. I don't feel very creative today, do you?' Jenna gave an angry little laugh.

Clare's round, babyish face creased into a worried frown—for the expense buying a ready-made pudding entailed. 'Oh. Good idea,' she rallied slowly. 'Actually, though, the way it's shaping up, we might not be needing any pud—or main course, for that matter. We've had two cancellations in the last hour.' She stared glumly at Jenna.

Jenna looked back at her sister-in-law with concern. 'Are you feeling all right?' she asked, genuinely worried. Clare was six months pregnant with her second child, and seemed to be getting more tired and more listless by the day. Not getting enough rest was only part of the problem; stress was the main reason, and they were all suffering from that—Jenna, Clare and Chris. Clare lifted a shoulder in a dispirited shrug. 'I'm a bit tired, that's all. The baby has been kicking, and Jodie has been a monster all afternoon. It's the weather getting to her, I suppose. I've only just managed to put her down for a nap. Just one of those days.' Clare's large soft blue eyes met Jenna's deep brown ones in a weary, rueful smile, then changed expression as they ran over Jenna's tightly drawn face, which was unnaturally white under the mass of dark curls.

'You don't look too good yourself,' she observed. 'Is anything the matter? Apart from the storm coming, I mean.'

Jenna gave a hasty shake of the head. 'I'm OK. I'll make us a cup of tea, shall I?' She filled the kettle and set it on the stove. 'You have a rest for a while; I'll just run around and close the shutters while the kettle boils.'

There was always a special feel about the island before a storm—this kind of storm; a slowly gathering one that gave hours of uneasy notice. It was the sort of storm Jenna hated most. The short, unexpected ones were better; they hit without warning and were gone in a flash, not giving her time to work up the uncontrollable tension that made the inside of her head feel so tight, she was afraid something was going to explode.

She raced down the long, wide veranda of the convict-built house, slamming the shutters of the four sets of windows that gave on to the veranda, then back inside the house she went into every room, checking the windows. They were all fastened; Clare had already seen to them, but in helpless compulsion Jenna went around all of them again. She always did that. It was stupid and irrational and there was nothing she could do about it; it didn't need a psychologist to explain that her fear of storms dated back to the death of her parents. They had been killed during a storm, when one of the hundred-foot pines had crashed down on to their car. Jenna had been seven; Christopher eleven. They had been waiting at home with their grandmother, and it was something that had transmitted itself from the old lady that night, rather than the actual death of her parents, that had stayed with Jenna all these years, the sense of impending disaster. In every storm her grandmother's white-faced, silent fear came back; in every storm, Jenna subconsciously waited for disaster.

Clare found her in the restaurant. 'I went around the windows before you came back. I knew you'd . . .'

'You know me,' Jenna cut her off with a jerky smile. 'Can't help myself.' They knew of her phobia, Clare, Chris and a few others, and tried to be tolerant and sympathetic, which only made Jenna feel even more of an idiot. Only Adam let his exasperation show, and Jenna knew that as soon as they were married he would pressure her into some sort of 'treatment'. Adam Nash was a doctor and would have loved to be a psychiatrist, but, unfortunately for him, the islanders didn't have enough neuroses to have made such a speciality pay.

'Was that the phone I heard a moment ago?' Jenna asked. 'Another cancellation, I suppose,' she guessed, accurately.

Clare nodded. 'The pensioner couple from up at the Lodge. They've decided not to risk venturing out tonight.'

'Wise of them,' Jenna returned with brittle approval. 'Is that the lot, then? Have they all cancelled now?'

'There's one booking left—a party of three,' Clare told her, trying to sound cheerful, as if three bodies in a room meant to hold fifty was something to be cheerful about.

'And what's the bet that they'll ring up at the last minute—if at all—to say they won't be coming, either? We may as well get in first and ring them to say we'll be closed tonight on account of the storm. What do you think?' Jenna looked at her sister-in-law expectantly.

Clare looked as if she didn't know what to think. 'Well . . . if you really think so. But what will Chris . . .'

Jenna cut her off with a sound of exasperation. 'Oh, who cares what Chris will say?' she muttered snappishly. Then, as Clare suddenly looked teary, she put an arm around her shoulders and gave it an abrupt squeeze. 'Why don't you go and lie down for a while? I'll look after Jodie when she wakes up.' Jenna wanted to be alone. Later, when the storm hit, she would be terrified to be left by herself for a single moment, but, just now, even Clare's undemanding presence was too taxing on her fraying nerves.

With Clare gone, Jenna moved edgily around the room, smoothing perfectly smooth tablecloths and straightening straightly laid cutlery.

It was a lovely room—two rooms, actually, made into one by the arch put into the wall between them. The larger area had been the former drawing-room of their grandmother's old home; the smaller, the dining-room. Both had the same moulded cornices and elegant fireplaces, and projected a graciousness that was not a common feature of the island's restaurants, which by and large tended to favour an overpowering mix of convict and *Bounty* memorabilia—both spurious, because Cone Island couldn't in all conscience lay any great claim to either. Its abortive penal settlement had lasted barely two years, while its tenuous *Bounty* connection was only via a handful of descendants of Pitcairn islanders who had come across from Norfolk Island at the turn of the century. Still, however remote, the islanders used their brush with history to bolster their growing tourist industry, and Jenna had to wonder if having some prints of poor old Captain Bligh and his *Bounty* might have helped to get their restaurant off the ground. It had become dismally obvious that they needed something.

The restaurant had been Chris's idea. Clare had been for it, too—as she was for all her husband's ideas, some of them positively hare-brained. Under the pressure of their combined enthusiasm, Jenna had allowed herself to be persuaded to turn part of their grandmother's house into a restaurant when Sarah Anderson had died four months ago and left them the house—and nothing else.

It had meant taking out a substantial loan to set it up, but, caught up in Chris and Clare's enthusiasm, she had really believed they could make a go of it. They might have too, if Clare hadn't turned out to be pregnant; if they had had enough funds in reserve to see them through the first teeth-cutting months; if Chris hadn't become sick of it all, worried for Clare and wanting out after barely two months, wanting to sell up everything, restaurant and house, to finance his latest idea of buying a small house for his family and using the rest of the money to buy into a cruiser to ferry tourists about.

Jenna had tried to persuade him to give the restaurant more time, convinced they could make it work despite the present, unpalatable fact that, if it wasn't for Chris's part-time job on one of the local fishing-trawlers, they would have been in more dire financial straits than they already were.

And then a week ago, Adam Nash had proposed, again, and Jenna had accepted. Now, the arrangement was that Adam would buy Chris out lock, stock and barrel after the wedding in two months' time. So Chris would have his money, and Jenna her restaurant.

'How convenient,' Clare had said with uncharacteristic tartness when Jenna told her their troubles would soon be over. And Chris had muttered he supposed they could struggle on another two months, but why the hell didn't Adam buy him out immediately, or at least after the official engagement party which was now only a week away? Jenna knew the answer to that but didn't want to think about it, let alone voice her suspicions to her brother.

Jodie woke, fretful and wanting her mother. Not

having the heart to wake Clare, Jenna took her niece into the kitchen and did her best to keep the fractious child occupied until Chris came home, late, tired and testy.

'Where's Clare?' were his first words.

Jenna smelt the beer on his breath and felt herself seize up with an anger she was finding harder and harder to suppress. The daily visits to the pub after work was Chris's way of reminding her he had washed his hands of the restaurant and resented every minute he was forced to put into his erstwhile 'baby'. Jenna could have hit him for his unreasonableness and wondered how she was going to stand another two months of it. 'Clare went to rest a few hours ago and fell asleep,' she told him tightly. 'There's no reason to wake her because we won't need her in the kitchen tonight. Most of the few bookings we had have cancelled, and there's only a party of three still on the books. With a bit of luck, they'll cancel too before the hour is out, so we might as well consider ourselves closed for the night. What do you say?' Jenna repeated the suggestion she had already made to Clare.

Chris gave her a grim smile. 'It's your idea to keep this wretched restaurant running instead of packing it in as I wanted to do, so you might show a little enthusiasm while you're about it,' he said in a flabbergasting display of reverse logic. The next thing he would be saying was that the restaurant had been all her idea in the first place. 'A party of three will at least cover the cost of the food that will otherwise go to waste, so you'd better keep your fingers crossed they turn up,' Chris finished with a growl, in a vile temper and on the look-out for a fight. Jenna recognised the signs only too well. She gritted her teeth and side-stepped the cue to a row.

'Why don't you take your bath and change now?' she suggested placatingly. 'I'll give Jodie her dinner and you can put her to bed, so we won't need to wake Clare at all. She's all right,' Jenna added firmly as the worried look sprang into Chris's eyes, deep, dark brown like her own. 'She's just tired, Chris, that's all.'

'She works too hard. She shouldn't be standing on her feet at the stove in her condition.'

What else would she be standing on if not her feet? Jenna wanted to retort. 'No, she shouldn't,' she agreed quickly to deflect her brother from this well-worn path to an argument.

'Yes, well, all right.' Chris pulled his horns in. 'Storm will hit in about an hour. Will you be all right?' he asked with a gruffness that held a grudging concern.

'Yes, of course I will,' Jenna reassured him briskly—and herself, while she was at it. 'I'll be fine, really I will. And anyway, it probably won't be much of a storm. Mr Young at the chemist was saying he thinks it will spend itself at sea somewhere near Norfolk Island, and we'll only get the tail end of it. We probably won't even notice it,' Jenna added with a shaky laugh as she lied to herself.

It hit while she was alone in the kitchen, stirring the lobster bisque. The party had arrived; 'two men, one woman,' Chris had muttered when he brought in their orders and hurried out again to play host/waiter, a role he had turned out to be rotten at, but since he couldn't cook there had not been anything else for him to do.

First came the blinding play of zigzagging streaks of light that turned the darkness outside the window into a blaze of white that seemed to burst physically into the room. And, almost at the same moment, there was a horrendous, ear-splitting crack of a gigantic whip. A fraction's pause, and the terrifying *son et lumière* performance repeated itself; again and again. Jenna stood stock still, momentarily stunned into stone, her mind seized into blank fright, then with the rush of wind and rain she came out of the trance, shaking so much she had to lurch over to the table and grab the edge of it to steady herself. She was making unconscious whimpering sounds like a terrified child when her brother burst in.

'Jenna, the soup, for heaven's sake. Oh, God!' Chris exclaimed as his eyes focused on her face and sized up the situation in a flash. 'Just sit down. I'll take over.'

'No! No.' Jenna's voice rose on a wave of hysteria. 'I'm all right, really I am. It was just the noise that frightened me. It's only the wind and rain now, and I'll be all right. You go back in there and I'll bring the soup out myself in a moment. Oh, and look in on Jodie, she may have wakened.' Jenna thought she was sounding amazingly calm, but strangely she didn't appear to be convincing Chris that she had everthing under control.

'I'll get Clare. She's with Jodie,' Chris muttered with weary resignation.

'No, don't! There's no need. Please, Chris,' Jenna pleaded, forcing herself back to the soup on the stove. It seemed madly important that she didn't succumb to her childish fears, didn't go to pieces for once.

Indecision all over his face, Chris dithered for a moment; the next, he rushed out again, leaving Jenna resolutely at the stove.

Five minutes later, Jenna carried the tray with its tureen of bisque through the swinging doors into the smaller section of the restaurant, across the corridor from the kitchen. Before her, the lovely, long, double room looked about as inviting as a scout hall with its sea of empty tables. The three guests were in the larger section by the fireplace; Chris was standing near by, looking as unlike a picture of the gracious host as you could possibly find.

Jenna started towards them, a glazed smile fixed on her face, then, as the man who had his back to her turned slightly, she caught his profile. Without conscious thought, she spun around and headed straight back to where she had come from.

Chris was on her heels by the time Jenna hurled herself into the kitchen. He snatched the tray from her hands. 'What the hell is going on?'

Jenna was so beside herself, she could barely speak. She stared at her brother in incredulous horror. 'How could you? How *could* you? Why didn't you tell me? How could you just let me walk in there like that?'

Chris looked flabbergasted. 'What are you talking about?'

'Drew Merrick! Drew Merrick! That's what I'm talking about,' Jenna hissed, her eyes raging wildly at her blank-faced brother.

'So what? What's he got to do with anything? What's got into you, Jenna?' Chris hissed back, angry and puzzled, and Jenna felt a wild, dangerous urge to shriek with laughter.

Never very interested in other people's business, Chris's self-absorption really had to take the cake; he would have to be about the only person on Cone Island not to know what Drew Merrick had to do with Jennifer Anderson. Only Chris could have let her walk into that restaurant without a word of warning.

'Pull yourself together, Jenna, for heaven's sake, and get the steaks started. I'll . . .' The rest of his words were lost in a new crash of thunder that boomed into the room. Chris shook his head in frustration and looked as if he was at the end of his tether as he left the room with the tray.

Jenna had long passed hers. Her nerves were shot to ribbons, and there seemed to be something crashing around inside her head that made it impossible to think straight. Since getting back from the township, where everybody had taken it that she would be so interested to hear Drew Merrick was back on the island, Jenna hadn't dared let herself think about him at all. And now he was here . . . in the restaurant . . . virtually in her home.

Two steaks Grand Marnier, one plain grilled. Jenna moved dazedly around the kitchen. If only she could think, if only the wind would stop for just one moment . . .

The steaks were on; at least she had managed that. She had taken the chocolate cheesecake out of the refrigerator and was lifting it out of its cardboard container when the intensified howl of wind sounded as if it was going to blow the solid sandstone house to pieces; a second later, the room plunged into darkness. Jenna didn't know what she did—screamed, she supposed; she knew she dropped the cake, because she saw it later trampled into the floor. Had she kept screaming in the dark until the disjointed sound of voices and running footsteps all converged in the kitchen? There was a gap in her mind that couldn't account for the time between the lights going out and the calm voice soothing her, as a comforting arm found her rigid shoulder in the darkness and held her tightly. Dazed and hysterical as she was, Jenna would have known that voice anywhere.

CHAPTER TWO

THE rest of the night was a blur. Jenna woke to the warm calm of the morning and thought she must have dreamt it all: the storm, the blackout and the chaos in the kitchen, with everybody stumbling in from everywhere—Clare from the bedroom with a screaming Jodie in her arms, Chris from wherever, Drew Merrick and his companions from the restaurant—all milling about, bumping into each other, except Jenna herself, who had stayed immobile under the arm around her shoulder which she knew belonged to Drew Merrick. Drew hadn't milled about, either.

Then Chris stumbled out to get the generator going and, with the lights on again, an edgy, embarrassed calm settled in, with Drew taking charge and making scrambled eggs for everyone—an incongruous short-order cook in his superbly tailored dark suit, whisking eggs and making toast, and yet, oddly, not looking funny, although Jenna remembered she had wanted to laugh. She hoped she hadn't, but couldn't be sure. What she could remember, though—and vividly— was the elegant blonde woman in the black dress, briskly giving Drew a helping hand, appearing quite at home and seeming to find nothing particularly odd about guests having to make their own supper.

The other man with them Jenna couldn't recall
saying anything as he scraped the cake off the floor
before disappearing—presumably back into the
restaurant. Jenna had sat there watching it all and
feeling utterly removed from the milling activity.
Afterwards, someone had taken her to her room.
Not someone. Drew Merrick. Jenna remembered
that and groaned aloud.

Of all the horrible things that could have
happened to her, she couldn't imagine anything
worse than Drew Merrick witnessing her hysterical
turn. Bad enough that he was back on the island;
bad enough that he had turned up in her house; but
to see her actually go to pieces, thrown into a panic
by a bit of lightning and thunder, and screaming in
the dark like a frightened child . . . It was
mortifying. Drew knew of the phobia she had had
from childhood, but to witness it now in a grown
woman . . . Jenna could have died.

She got up and put on the shabby, faded cotton
robe which was coming apart under the arms where
she had patched and repatched it to stave off the
inevitable day when it would take its rightful place
in the rag-bag where it should have gone years
ago—along with most of her other clothes. And
where would that leave her? Walking around
starkers, that's where, Jenna muttered to herself,
angry that something as trivial as a ragged robe
should be grating so much of late. The reason was
Adam, and the wedding. Well, he would have to
take her as he found her, ragged robe and all, except
that Jenna knew he would immediately send her off

to buy herself some clothes, and she couldn't bear to think about that humiliating prospect. Not this morning.

The large house was very silent—empty silent. Chris had left for work hours ago; she vaguely remembered the sound of the car engine penetrating her sleep. Clare seemed to have taken herself and Jodie off somewhere too, knowing Jenna wouldn't feel like facing anyone before her embarrassment had worn off. Her bare feet silent on the cool stone floor, Jenna pattered through the empty house into the kitchen and was well into the room before she saw Drew at the dresser, his back to her, telephone at his ear. The moment's stunned indecision cost Jenna her getaway. Drew turned suddenly, reaching out a hand in a jerky gesture that might have meant 'hello' or 'don't go', and said sharply into the phone, 'Not good enough, Mitchell. You'll have to do better than that. What about Tuesday?' He kept his eyes focused on Jenna while scowling at whatever was being said into his ear.

While her first thought had been to turn tail and run, the one following on its heels was that Drew Merrick making business calls in her kitchen was the absolute limit, and she was going to tell him so in no uncertain terms. Gripping the lapels of her thin robe tightly together, Jenna remained where she was, glowering at him.

'Yes, OK, Wednesday, then. And make sure your chaps are over first thing this afternoon to see to the temporary repairs.' Drew put the phone down. 'Here you are, then. Did you manage to get a decent sleep?' Deftly, Drew got in first, forestalling Jenna's attack; the slow, easy smile made her grip the lapels tighter.

'Come and sit down. The coffee is still hot,' Drew invited, and rendered her momentarily speechless by the presumption. 'I stayed the night—we all did,' he ran on, chattily. 'Your brother insisted, what with the storm and everything. The others left with him an hour or so ago.'

'Then you should have left with them!' Jenna launched into the delayed attack at last. 'In case you haven't noticed, the storm is over and I'm sure you'd be more comfortable attending to your pressing business matters from your own hotel.' Her tone dripped sarcasm.

'Correction, *your* business matters, Jenna.' Drew's voice had taken on an icy edge and, as Jenna frowned her incomprehension, his smile returned with derision in it. 'It's you who haven't noticed yet that part of your roof came off last night, and I'm here now because I promised Chris I'd try and organise something with Mitchell as soon as the telephone came back on. Which I have, and not without difficulty, I might add. It seems that half the houses on the island were deroofed last night, and Mitchell's men are going to have their work cut out replacing them all. I'm sorry if I've given the impression I've been making free with your telephone,' Drew added snidely, but Jenna was already half-way out the door.

She did a rapid circuit of the house, coming across the scattering of broken tiles on the ground by the veranda outside the restaurant. Peering up, she could see a couple of corresponding gaps in the roof to account for them. A nuisance, but hardly a major catastrophe. Relieved, she went back inside the house.

Mug of coffee in hand, Drew was leaning against the waist-high row of cupboards by the sink. The shaft of sunlight streaming in through the window behind him caught the top of his head, picking out the sun-bleached strands in the thick, dark hair and giving them coppery highlights—the sort women paid a fortune for at exclusive hair salons. His skin was very tanned above the whiteness of the slightly crumpled shirt; the several undone buttons revealed the tan dipping down into his chest, while the rolled-up sleeves showed hard-muscled brown arms. Drew looked lean and healthy and impossibly handsome, even with a night's stubble on his chin.

'Satisfied?' he smiled mockingly, the drawled question ambiguous, since it might as easily have applied to her blatantly staring appraisal of him as to her tour of inspection of the damage. Whichever, Drew had the arrogant self-assurance of someone who had the upper hand in this encounter.

Damn it, she was playing this all wrong. Jenna checked the bad-tempered retort and shrugged carelessly. 'The damage doesn't appear at all extensive, but thank you for organising Mitchell for us,' she said, dismissively, as if addressing a handyman who had meant well but had exceeded his authority. She had the satisfaction of seeing Drew's eyes narrow with anger at the carefully administered snub. 'And yes, I will have some coffee, thanks,' Jenna added, all airiness. She was pleased with herself for managing to hit the right tone of voice—the one that put Drew Merrick in his place. Going to the table, she pulled out a chair and sat down and watched him pour a coffee for her at the bench. 'Thank you,' she said graciously when Drew brought it over and put it down in front of her. She met his eyes in an ingenuous stare. 'Well, this is a surprise, Drew. What's brought you back to the island? Homesickness?' Jenna asked brightly, and gave a brittle little laugh at her own facetious suggestion. There was no love lost between Drew and the island—islanders, rather—and he had sworn a long time ago that he wouldn't set foot back on the island if he could help it.

'Business,' Drew mutterd shortly, and remained standing at the edge of the table, a closed, angry expression on his face.

Jenna laughed up at him. 'Of course, what else? Silly of me not to have guessed. But why in person, Drew? Surely you could buy up the few bits of island you don't already own from your regular safe distance of Sydney or London—or wherever it is you busy tycoons operate from. We can hardly keep up with your whereabouts these days,' she mocked with a wide smile, then flicked it off like a light as she realised she had just given away the fact that his whereabouts were of interest to the island. To her.

The hard line of Drew's mouth relaxed into a sardonic curve. 'Rankles, doesn't it?' he said softly. 'You're all green with envy, and not to put too fine a point on it, hate my guts for the success I've become.' He said it with the smile in place, but the malice came through sharp and clear, and Jenna was taken aback by it.

'Nonsense, Drew, you're exaggerating,' she rallied with mock severity. 'We're all very pleased for you—our own local boy making good and all that,' she put in, trying to make a joke of it, and thought, yes, he's right—the whole island is riddled with envy of this powerful, ruthless businessman who had once been Andy Merrick, the grocer's son and an outsider in the island's tightly knit, snob-ridden 'old family' society run by her own grandmother. It was those self-same 'old families' who envied him the most now and felt the most threatened since Drew had become such an economic force on the island.

'And does it make you feel good now—owning half the island . . . among other things, of course?' Jenna sounded flippant, but was aware that deep down, she was nervously curious for a glimpse of the man behind the hard, handsome face, and perhaps for a glimpse, too, of the angry young man she had been so crazy about and who had gone away and married somebody else.

'As a matter of fact, it does,' Drew replied carelessly, ambling back to the bench and pouring himself another coffee. Jenna took a sip of hers in silence.

Drew looked across the room at her and lifted an eyebrow. 'Well, is that it?'

'What?' Jenna asked sharply.

'Is that the end of the interview, or is there any thing else you'd like to know? I thought perhaps you'd been conducting an in-depth interview for the local rag.'

Jenna flushed. 'I was only expressing polite interest,' she muttered huffishly.

'Ah, so that's what it was.' Drew returned to the table with his coffee and sat down. 'And what about you, Jenna?' The reach for her hand across the table was so unexpected and so quick that Jenna had no time to pull it out of range. Holding her fingers in almost a crunch, Drew lifted the hand up and examined it with spurious interest. 'What, no engagement ring?' He raised his eyes to her face. 'You weren't wearing a ring last night, either.'

Jenna yanked her hand out of his slackened grip with a wrench. 'I hadn't realised you'd added seeing in the dark to the long list of your remarkable talents,' she retorted, giving the hand an angry rub, as if to rub away the sensation of warmth left by the contact of his hand.

'Oh, I tend to notice things that interest me,' Drew drawled airily, 'and it wasn't dark for very long, was it? But why no ring, Jenna?' he persisted. 'I undestood you and the very worthy Dr Nash were engaged. Again.' The last word was underlined with heavy sarcasm.

Jenna glowered her fury at him and said nothing, then, aware she was still rubbing away at her hand, dropped both hands to her lap.

'Incidentally, I spotted your fiancé making a dash for it across the main street yesterday. He really shouldn't be exerting himself like that with his growing weight problem, you know.' Drew tut-tutted like a disapproving old woman.

Jenna's endurance of his mockery ended with a snap. 'Shut up!' she burst out like a pettish child, and then, as Drew eased his chair away from the table and lazily stretched out his long, lean legs in front of him, she ran her eyes up and down them, utterly unthinkingly. The next second she tore her gaze away in a violent fluster.

Drew crossed one leg casually over the other. 'So what's the arrangement? A ceremonial presentation of *the* ring to cap off the official announcement of this latest engagement? Next Saturday, isn't it?' He nodded in satisfied answer to his own question. 'The Nashes have always had a rather unfortunate tendency to stand on ceremony, haven't they?'

He was maddeningly right. About the business of the ring—Adam's ridiculous idea. About the Nashes. About Adam's slight gain of weight, for that matter. 'It's none of your business,' Jenna muttered angrily, her eyes glaring dislike at him.

'I was only expressing polite interest.' Drew mimicked her words with a smug smile.

Jenna shoved her chair back with a scrape and jumped up. 'I'm very busy today, Drew, so if you wouldn't mind leaving . . . now.' This encounter had gone on long enough, and Jenna felt in real danger of losing her cool and her dignity.

'Surely not yet, not when we've still got so much catching up to do after all these years?' Drew affected injured surprise, but stood up too. Then, as he didn't move, that left them standing there, face to face, and much too close for Jenna's nerves. She hurriedly sat down again.

Drew flicked her a grin as he sauntered away from the table, not going anywhere in particular, but simply roaming around the kitchen. Jenna watched, seething. 'So how's the restaurant business?'

She would have loved to tell him some outrageous lie—the restaurant was booming, packed to the rafters every night—only she knew that a businessman like Drew Merrick could probably estimate to the last cent how much they were making—losing rather—every night.

'We're getting by,' she mumbled reluctantly. Even that was a lie, and she knew Drew recognised it for one. The dark brows shot up quizzically, goading her into lying more rashly. 'Last night was just the storm keeping people away. We had a lot of cancellations.'

'Then you must have been having a lot of unseasonal storms lately,' Drew commented drily, and glanced around the kitchen—a professional glance, taking in the shabby walls crying out for a coat of paint, the rickety cupboards. He flicked an eye over the brand-new industrial cooker—an outlandish extravagance and, in hindsight, an utter waste of money. He brought his eyes back to her. 'So she left you with nothing in the end,' he said expressionlessly, although there was something like pity in his eyes. Unwelcome.

Jenna turned her head away abruptly.

'I'm sorry about your grandmother.' Drew

offered the trite condolence without the slightest attempt to make it sound anything more than lip-service to convention, and Jenna swung her face back to him so violently that a muscle in her neck protested in pain.

'No, you're not! You're not the least bit sorry, Drew Merrick. You couldn't stand my grandmother, and you might have the decency not to pretend otherwise now that she's dead.'

Drew's features seized up into an instant scowl. 'I was not pretending anything. You're perfectly right; I couldn't stand your grandmother—nor she me, if you remember,' he said tightly through thin lips, and turned away from her, transferring his attention to the surface of the cooker and peering down at it as if he found it of consuming interest. Jenna studied his rigid back. Drew Merrick, ashamed of his display of callousness? Ashamed was too extreme a word; uncomfortable perhaps, and she struck while she had the chance.

'Well, it's been nice of you to look us up,' she said patronisingly, her grandmother's maliciously gracious drawl coming right out of her mouth. It was uncanny, and all it would have needed was the 'Andy' to complete the snub. She saw the back of Drew's suntanned neck below the hairline turn a dark red under the tan. He had not missed the tone of voice either, and it had stung. Really stung. He turned around slowly and had apparently used the few seconds to arrange his expression into a stony mask; his eyes were icy.

Her face very hot, Jenna stood up. 'I didn't mean

. . . I'm sorry,' she blurted agitatedly

The corner of Drew's mouth tilted in a bitter semi-smile. 'For what? Being Sarah Anderson's granddaughter?' He gave a low growl of a laugh. 'I'm sure you've nothing to be sorry about, Jenna; your grandmother would be proud of the way you've learn to put the local riff-raff in their places.'

Jenna's brief moment of shame flared into a heated confusion at his contempt. 'She never . . . I never . . .' she mumbled, without knowing what she wanted to say.

Drew took stock of her confusion with faintly amused interest. 'Mind you,' he continued, 'I imagine it might be a bit disconcerting for your customers. Do you make them use the tradesmen's entrance, too?' he asked, the faint, wry smile in place, but with the ice still in his eyes.

Jenna knew what he was getting at: her grandmother had never let Drew into the house, always insisting he used the back door when he came to deliver the groceries after school. Jenna had been very young then, eight or nine, and Drew already about sixteen. It must have been humiliating for him. 'You really hated her, didn't you?' Jenna said, shock in her voice, and then added in a harsh, childish spurt, 'You're probably glad she's dead. You must have been wishing it for years.'

Drew snorted. 'I haven't exactly spent my time away sticking pins into a voodoo doll of your old gran, if that's what you're implying, but it's true, I'm not particularly sorry she's finally gone—and I doubt anyone else is, either.'

Jenna went rigid with fury. 'How dare you? How dare you speak of my grandmother like that? She was a helpless and very sick old lady—dying, and she needed me.'

Drew laughed in her face. 'As helpless as a tarantula, and so sick she was chopping wood the day she died. Or is that highly entertaining story apocryphal?' The savage mirth went out of Drew's face, leaving it tight and angry and almost ugly in the dislike that projected from it. He said, with slow, cold emphasis, 'Sarah Anderson was a selfish, nasty old woman, clambering on to her deathbed every time it remotely looked like you might actually stand up to her and make a decision about your own life— what *you* wanted to do and *who* you wanted to do it with. And you needn't stand there blazing your eyes at me, because you know every callous word I'm saying is no more than the truth.'

This was it, and Jenna had known they would get to this point sooner or later; every word of heated exchange from the moment she had walked into the kitchen had been no more than pussyfooting towards this inevitable moment when the bitter past—hers, Drew's—was to be thrown on to the carving board, with the knives out and recriminations at the ready. She felt her heart thumping away in heavy, out-of-rhythm thumps that made her breathless. A tiny nerve above the left corner of Drew's mouth had started to twitch, and she realised that Drew, too, knew they had reached the point of no return.

Neither of them had heard a car draw up, and the child's appearance took them by surprise and

had the effect of momentarily disorientating both of
them. Jenna's first reaction was a sharp feeling of
angry disappointment that she had been cheated out
of the showdown, and then a wave of pure relief
swept through her.

'Jodie, darling,' she began brightly, making a
move towards the child who stood looking at the
adults, her eyes moving from one to the other. Then,
ignoring Jenna, she made a beeline for Drew with all
the fervour of greeting an old friend, never mind
that he was of one night's standing.

'Come ow . . . show . . . ow.' She clutched hold of
Drew's hand, excitedly intent on impressing the
urgency of something upon him. Drew was laughing
down at her as Clare came into the kitchen. She gave
Jenna a cursory smile and focused a large, warm one
on Drew.

Drew gave Jodie's head a light pat as he returned
Clare's smile. 'I get the impression that something
frightfully important is afoot. Could you interpret
for me?' he appealed to Clare, all masculine
helplessness and charm you could have scraped off
with a trowel, and Clare melted so visibly that it
made Jenna almost nauseous.

What a con artist! Any idiot could have figured
out that Jodie wanted to take him outside and show
him something.

'Jodie, don't be a nuisance, darling,' Clare
reproved the child with a silly giggle. 'Mr Merrick is
too busy to go out and see your bike. It's her
birthday today,' she explained to Drew, 'and Judy,
my sister, has just given her a tricycle. I've left it

outside for the moment—that's what she wants to show you, but you needn't . . .'

'But I'd love to see it,' Drew exclaimed, and really sounded as if he had been waiting a lifetime for the sight of a child's tricycle. 'Let's go and look at it now, shall we?' Good-naturedly, he allowed himself to be tugged out the door by a frantically excited Jodie. Clare beamed warmly after them.

'I forgot that it's today. I'm sorry,' Jenna said brusquely, aware that she had committed a sin in Clare's eyes. 'I did mean to get her something in the town yesterday afternoon, but with the storm coming and everything else——' hearing Drew Merrick was back on the island . . . 'I'll get her something this afternoon,' Jenna promised contritely. 'Did Judy drive you back just now?'

'Yes. Chris took us over there on his way to work, after he'd dropped off that couple at their hotel.' Clare moved to the window. 'I thought you and Drew might want . . .' She broke off, and broke into a radiant, gratified smile as her attention focused outside the window. Jodie's audible squeals of laughter told of great fun and games going on. 'Oh, do come and look, Jenna,' Clare urged with a delighted laugh. 'She's trying to make Drew sit on her bike and he's . . .'

'I'm going to get dressed,' Jenna cut her off rudely, not moving an inch towards the window.

Clare threw her a glance and only now seemed to take in what Jenna was wearing. Or not wearing. Jenna could read the unspoken censure in her sister-in-law's po-faced look very clearly: how could you be lounging about in that tatty old thing with a man like Drew Merrick around?

How, indeed? Jenna met Clare's disapproving eyes and gave a careless shrug, then she moved towards the door leading into the corridor.

'But won't you want to see Drew out?' Clare asked in sharp surprise. 'He might think you're being rude,' she called out as Jenna disappeared through the doorway.

'He might,' Jenna called back tartly from the corridor.

She took her time taking a shower, and then, after she had dressed in jeans and a long-sleeved, cherry-red top, she still had to sit about in her room for ages before she heard Drew drive off in the hire-car he had arrived in last evening. He must have stayed to have yet another coffee, or three, and all for the sake of ingratiating himself with Clare—which had been a pushover through the child. But Jenna couldn't for the life of her fathom why he would want to bother. Clare had no interest in any man other than Chris, and, pregnant or otherwise, would hardly have been Drew Merrick's type, anyway. The woman last night, whoever she was, was Drew's type to a T, or what Jenna sourly imagined must now be his type—super-cool, understatedly elegant and as sophisticated as they made them.

She couldn't be his wife—not yet at any rate; that much Jenna knew, because the place would have been abuzz for weeks if Drew Merrick had gone and got himself married again. News of that sort would have hit the remote island with the force of a major cyclone. Andy Merrick had turned into their local celebrity years ago and, for all their hostility towards him, the islanders were almost obsessively fascinated by him.

But why had Drew come back? Now? Now, of all times, when the past was just about to really become the past and Jenna had accepted that her future was with Adam Nash and this beautiful, bigoted, stifling little dot in the Pacific. Drew could not have chosen a worse time if he had tried—if he had sat down and deliberately worked out the best way of paying her back for what she had done to him. It had to be a coincidence, but his visit could mean trouble if she wasn't careful. And she hadn't been careful. Back there in the kitchen, before Jodie had interrupted, she had almost fallen into the trap of raking over the past, taking the lid off Pandora's box. Jenna shuddered at the thought.

CHAPTER THREE

'HE'S really wonderful with children, isn't he?' Clare remarked, oozing a mushy gratitude towards the absent Drew when Jenna rejoined her in the kitchen.

'Oh, wonderful,' muttered Jenna through her teeth. She was given a long, reproachful look, which she ignored; instead, she set about getting out some bread for toast. Breakfast was long overdue, and she was starving.

'I thought you and Drew were old friends, but you don't sound as if you like him very much,' Clare said after a little silence, and in the sort of neutral I'm-only-making-a-comment voice which didn't fool Jenna for a moment. She could recognise fishing when she heard it. Clare was well up in island gossip, and would have been dying of curiosity about what had transpired between Jenna and Drew.

Jenna had no intention of satisfying it. 'That's probably because I don't,' she returned with a discouraging snap, and went on making her toast. 'Shall we start going through the menu for tonight?' she suggested briskly after she had settled herself at the table.

Clare looked at her oddly. 'But didn't Drew tell you?'

'Tell me what?'

'That the restaurant will have to close.'

'What?' Jenna barked, and could have sworn Clare was rather pleased at having produced such a reaction out of her. 'What on earth are you talking about?' she demanded, fixing Clare with a glare that wiped the smugness off her sister-in-law's face.

'The roof, Jenna,' Clare started to explain hastily. 'It came off last night—part of it, and . . .'

'I know that,' Jenna interrupted shortly. 'A few tiles, that's all, hardly . . .'

Clare was shaking her head. 'The rain damaged the ceiling in the restaurant. It's not safe, Jenna. Drew said . . .'

'Oh, rot his socks!' Jenna burst out petulantly.

'Well, it's not his fault, is it?' Clare rallied to his defence, a little pink spot appearing in each pale cheek. 'And Chris had a look at it too before we left this morning, and he . . .'

'Yes, all right, all right, I believe you.' Jenna cut off the explanation with surly resignation. 'How long do we have to stay closed? Did Drew decide that for us, too?' she asked sarcastically, mainly to give vent to her frustration in the face of the inevitable.

'I thought he would have told you,' Clare began, again with that faint smugness, as if she knew something Jenna didn't—until she read the look in Jenna's eyes. 'Until Mitchell's men turn up to fix it,' she said grudgingly, 'and I don't know when that will be because Drew . . .'

'Wednesday,' Jenna told her tersely, remembering Drew's discussion on the telephone. She gave a sudden, unamused laugh. 'Well, kiddo, it looks as though we're going to have ourselves a holiday, like it or not. And what's a few more hundred dollars down the drain?' Jenna stood up and took her cup and plate to the sink, then remained standing at the window, watching Jodie energetically, if not very effectively, trying to get some speed out of her little trike.

'Jenna.' Clare's voice was odd.

When she didn't continue, Jenna turned to her expectantly. Clare was chewing nervously on her lower lip. 'I just wondered . . .'

'What?' Jenna prompted impatiently.

'Er . . . what you and Drew talked about. I mean, did you talk about anything . . . special? Discuss anything?' she asked disjointedly, and she went red in the face as Jenna stared at her, more in amazement than in anger at this blatant prying.

'No,' Jenna said coldly, 'we did not.'

Clare went even redder, if that was possible. 'I'm sorry. I wasn't prying, really I wasn't. I mean, I didn't mean to. What I meant was . . .'

The telephone rang at that moment, putting an end to Clare's incoherent non-explanation. Jenna went over to the phone and picked it up. 'Good morning, Grandma's Kitchen,' she said curtly, her puzzled eyes still on Clare's red face.

'It's afternoon actually, darling,' Adam chuckled on the other end of the line.

Mechanically, Jenna glanced at her watch. 'So it is. It seems time flies even when you're not having fun. What is it, Adam?'

Some of the warmth went out of Adam's voice at her abrupt tone. 'Am I interrupting something? I only rang to check how you all came through the storm last night, but I won't hold you up if . . .'

'You're not interrupting anything, Adam.' Jenna was instantly contrite. 'And everything is fine here. Well, not quite,' she amended. 'I'm afraid we have to close for a couple of nights because some tiles came off last night, and apparently the rain has done some damage to the ceiling in the restaurant. Nothing major, but we still have to close.'

'Very wise. You can't take unnecessary risks,' Adam said approvingly. He was nothing if not a cautious man; sometimes Jenna found that irritating. 'What a pity I'm on call nights this week, otherwise we could have used your time off to see more of each other than we seem to manage these days.'

'Never mind, darling, can't be helped,' Jenna returned lightly, and was conscious that she was just that little bit relieved that Adam was on night-call. Pre-wedding tension, jitters, whatever, and hadn't she heard somewhere that all engaged couples went through a stage of finding each other's company rather a strain?

'I'll just have to be satisfied having you to lunch tomorrow, won't I? Oh, before I hang up, did you know Drew Merrick was back on the island?' Adam's attempt at by-the-way casualness didn't come off. The question came over as if it were directed to a hostile witness by a prosecuting counsel.

After a slight pause, Jenna said evenly, 'Yes. He was here last night. In the restaurant. With some friends,' she over-explained jerkily, and then was appalled at the mischievous urge she had to add, that he had stayed the night. She resisted the urge, and waited for Adam to say something.

Adam only said, 'I'll see you tomorrow,' and hung up without giving her time to even say goodbye.

'Damn Drew Merrick!' Jenna muttered angrily as she replaced the receiver.

Clare lifted her head from the magazine she had been idly flipping through, and looked at Jenna curiously.

Jenna flushed. 'Haven't you ever heard of privacy?' she snapped, and flung herself out of the room in a whirl of agitated bad temper, returning a moment later to let fly with, 'I'm going into town now—just so you don't die of curiosity, wondering where I've gone.' It was uncalled for and made Jenna feel a heel to see Clare's face fall into a pre-tears crumple. 'Oh, damn Drew Merrick,' she muttered to herself again as she stormed off to her car.

She spotted the trio—Drew, the woman and the fair-haired man—turning into the main street from the arcade ahead; saw them first, which meant she was able to duck into the nearest shop for cover, a café, as it happened, where she took a seat facing the window, ordered a coffee and prepared to sit out ten minutes or so to give them time to disappear.

She hadn't thought to ask Drew how long he
intended to stay on the island; a regrettable
oversight, but no doubt Clare had elicited that piece
of information from her new-found hero, and Jenna
would have to ask her if she wanted to know how
long she was destined to be on her guard, playing
hide-and-seek every time she went into town.

It was a quarter past two. The coffee lounge was
still full—tourists, predominantly retired couples
and a sprinkling of patently obvious honeymooners,
which was par for the course. The island was not
exactly a Club Med and, apart from families who
came during school holidays, retired people and
honeymooners from mainland Australia were the
mainstay of the island's growing tourist trade.

Jenna cast a speculative eye over them as she
sipped her coffee, and wondered why they found it
so hard to find their way to Grandma's Kitchen,
which made her remember that she had also
forgotten to ask Drew about Mitchell's quote for the
repairs. Whatever it was, they wouldn't be able to
pay outright, and would have to slide even further
into the red. The bank manager would have another
fit. Jenna sighed wearily, paid for the coffee and
went out.

There was no sign of Drew or his friends and,
feeling safe again, Jenna hurried across the street to
the toy shop to look for some inexpensive thing to
buy for Jodie, a colourful rag clown perhaps, or a
small doll

Her mind on dolls, she walked into the toy shop;
in the same moment, the woman standing at the doll

section lifted her eyes to the door. There was a brief frown across the beautifully made-up features, then a flicker of recognition, followed by a smile and a small wave of the hand that wasn't holding the doll.

'Hello, again,' Drew's elegant blonde called out with surprising friendliness. And she looked as elegant in daylight as she had the night before, dressed with casual sophistication in light-coloured suede slacks and matching jacket over a turquoise silk shirt. Her age Jenna put at early thirties, and she was childishly pleased to note the laugh lines around the blue eyes when she reluctantly joined her; short of blatantly ignoring her, there wasn't much else Jenna could have done.

'What do you think of this one?' the woman asked, holding out the doll for Jenna's inspection.

Several people were dotted around the shop, but there was no Drew Merrick; a frantic flick of the eye had reassured Jenna of that. Relieved, she examined the doll. 'It's lovely. Who are you buying it for?'

'For Drew,' the woman laughed, a pleasant, friendly sound. 'To give to your little niece,' she added with another laugh. 'It's her birthday today, I understand. Have you come to look for something, too?'

Jenna suddenly went rigid at the sound of the voice and laugh that came from somewhere behind the shoulder-high display of dolls beside them. She darted an agitated glance at the shelves, too high to peer over; she didn't need to, anyway.

'They're down on the floor, testing out a train-set,' the blonde smiled indulgently. 'Small boys, the pair of them. They never grow up, do they?'

Jenna supposed she was expected to answer something conventionally arch at the silliness of grown men playing with trains; all she could manage was a hasty jerk of a smile, too distracted to think of a rejoinder.

'I think I . . .' She broke off as Drew's deep laugh wafted up from behind the wall of dolls. 'I really must be going,' Jenna said, stupidly, since she had just come in, but she didn't get the chance to bolt. There was a flash of movement in the range of her left eye as Drew's head and shoulders materialised on the other side of the display, his companion popping up a moment later, and there she was, trapped among an array of dolls in Mrs Ellison's toy shop.

Drew had shaved and changed into some casual clothes. The grey and blue top, which was all Jenna could see, looked Italian and softly expensive; not a single gold chain around his neck for her to mentally sneer at. It was no consolation knowing Drew would have been as likely to have a tiara perched on his head as bedecked with trendy gold chains. Jenna felt like a country bumpkin beside this group of elegant, sophisticated people.

If Drew was surprised to see her, he didn't show it; he did look a little bit sheepish though, and to her own surprise Jenna took the initiative—tartly. 'Planning a takeover of the island's railway network?' she gibed with an arch lift of a long, strongly defined eyebrow.

Drew laughed at the snipe after a fraction's pause; Mrs Ellison's stock of train-sets was as close as the island came to having a railway system.

The others laughed, too. 'That's an idea, Drew. We'll have to put it to the board.' The fair man grinned at Jenna, then they both came around the display shelving.

'I don't believe we had any introductions last night,' Drew said casually. 'Jenna, this is Michael.' Jenna and the man exchanged slight nods. 'And this is Jessica Fenwick.'

Jenna nodded again. Other than the names, Drew's introduction gave nothing away.

'Jenna and I are old friends,' Drew went on, meeting Jenna's eyes with a wry smile; gauging how that outrageous lie went over?

Jenna looked back blandly and let it pass.

'Did you know your niece has been dying for a train-set, all her life, she told me? That would make it three whole years.' Drew chuckled at Jessica, then glanced at the doll she was still holding. 'Very nice, Jess. A doll was second choice to the train-set, but I rather suspect the child would give her entire set of milk teeth for both.'

'Then I hope you're not about to do anything so silly as to indulge her. She has enough toys already,' Jenna told him crossly. It was not really true; Jodie probably had fewer toys than most children, but it was not for Drew Merrick to remedy that situation with glad-handed largesse.

'Why don't you get her the doll, then?' Jessica suggested brightly—and innocently, Jenna supposed, since the woman could not have had any idea that the cost of a doll like that would have kept Jenna's car running for months and probably bought it a new battery as well.

'I haven't decided on anything yet,' Jenna muttered quite rudely in her embarrassment, tearing her eyes away from Jessica and the doll. 'I just popped in to look around.' What she had had in mind had been a doll like the little one on the second-from-top row of the display, though she would have been mortified to pick it up and check the price-tag in front of them. In front of Drew Merrick, who could probably have bought the entire contents of the shop out of his office petty-cash box. Was she being hyper-sensitive? Drew knew she was as poor as a church mouse, and keeping up appearances had been her grandmothers's preoccupation, not hers. But Jenna had her pride. She smiled tightly at Michael, since her eyes fell on him as the least threatening of the three. 'I must be going. Nice to have met you.'

'Oh, but perhaps you would join us for a drink or a coffee before you go home.' It was Jessica who came out with the invitation—unexpected, and very telling of her relationship with Drew—obviously a close one to allow her to issue invitations on his behalf. But Jenna had already put two and two together on that score, so why did this confirmation of her arithmetic come as such a curiously unpleasant surprise?

Jenna was slow with her smile, and when it came she was conscious of its being fatuously brilliant.

'How very kind of you, but I'm afraid I can't. And I've only just had one—a coffee, I mean,' she fairly gushed, taking care not to catch Drew's eye. 'And I do need to get back to the house. The restaurant, you know, we . . .' About to blurt out something about needing to start preparing for dinner, she caught the lie back in the nick of time before she made a complete fool of herself.

'Yes, of course. I'd forgotten. You're expecting some workman over to see to your roof, aren't you? Drew mentioned it. A terrible nuisance for you.' Jessica was all understanding and concern.

And what else had Drew 'mentioned' to her? Jenna was nodding mechanically. 'A terrible nuisance,' she heard herself repeating like a parrot, turning to Michael again because she was starting to feel glassy-eyed in the attempt at looking blandly at Drew's disconcertingly friendly girlfriend.

'Well, we shall have to make a date to get together in the next couple of days—your brother, too. There's no reason we can't combine business with pleasure, is there?'

'Jessica, I don't think we should hold up Jenna any longer,' Drew broke in with a sharpness that brought a puzzled frown to Jessica's face. He put what could have been taken as a restraining hand on her arm. 'We'd better go and settle with Mrs Ellison for that,' he said, less sharply, nodding at the doll, 'or she'll begin to think we're planning to abscond with it. Clare won't really mind if I get Jodie the train-set as well, will she?' He addressed Jenna with an appealing smile that she was too distracted to resent, because her mind was still on Jessica's last perplexing remark, and Drew's equally perplexing reaction to it.

'No, I suppose not,' she replied in a preoccupied murmur.

'Good. Catch up with you later.' Drew gave her a nod and walked off towards the counter. Ironically, given her anxiety to get away from him, Jenna felt herself dismissed, and didn't like it.

Flashing a perfunctory smile at Jessica Fenwick and the ever-silent Michael, she hurried out of the shop, feeling her nerves could have done with Jessica's suggested drink after being put through that little episode.

It would have been more convenient to buy a picture book at the toy shop, but Jenna trekked up two blocks to buy it at the bookstore, virtually choosing the first one she picked up. Whatever present she gave now was destined to fade into insignificance once Jodie's innocently greedy little eyes lit on Drew's excessive offerings. The thought rankled. Amazing how much friction Drew could generate without even trying. Heaven help her, when he really set to work! And something was afoot; something Jessica Fenwick and even Clare knew about.

Chris's car was already in the drive when Jenna reached the house. He finished work early on Saturday but rarely came straight home, usually preferring to spend the extra time at the pub, and this deviation from habit only increased Jenna's suspicions.

'Is there something going on that I should know about?' she asked challengingly from the doorway of the room Chris and Clare used as their sitting-room. They were sitting side by side on the sofa, and both started in surprise. Clare stole a guilty glance at her husband and let out a nervous little giggle.

'What are you talking about?' Chris countered belligerently, taking a sip from the beer can in his hand; there were two more cans on the coffee-table in front of him.

'Oh, Chris,' Clare began whiningly.

'I'm talking about some very odd things that people have been coming out with—you, Clare, asking me what Drew and I talked about this morning, then that Jessica Fenwick, whoever she might be, gushing on in town today about how we must all get together to combine business with pleasure. What business, I want to know.' So much for the nonchalance she had planned: avoid a confrontation at all costs. Jenna was in no mood for pussyfooting, and if she needed confirmation of her suspicions that something was going on behind her back, she had it in her brother's surly, handsome face. Chris stared pugnaciously at the wall in front of him, refusing to meet Jenna's eye.

'Drew has made an offer for Chris's share of the restaurant—and the house, too,' Clare volunteered, making her voice all eager and bright, and looking at Jenna with a bright little smile to match. 'Come and sit down, Jenna. We were just talking about it, weren't we, Chris?'

Jenna let out a laugh of shocked disbelief, an

ugly sound that made Clare hurriedly drop her eyes
to her lap. Jenna came into the room slowly and sat
down in one of her grandmother's ancient, oversized
chintz armchairs, its pattern faded beyond
recognition, and as shabby as everything else in the
house—spanking-new restaurant excepted.

'And when did this interesting development
occur?' she asked, very evenly, quite pleasantly, in
fact—dangerously so, but Clare missed the danger
signal and broke into a relieved smile.

'Last night, after you'd gone to bed. Drew talked
to us.' Clare glanced at Chris, who didn't look at
her; he looked bored. Jenna knew the look well; it
was not boredom, it was Chris's obstinate, pig-
headed look.

'He . . . Drew said he'd talk to you about it this
morning, and that's why I asked.' Clare's voice
faltered and trailed away as Jenna's suppressed fury
finally registered.

Jenna kept her eyes fixed unwaveringly on her
brother's face, silently challenging him to meet her
eyes. In the end, Chris turned to her, and they
looked at each other in a long, hard glare.

'You're not going to put a spanner in the works,
Jenna. I won't let you,' Chris said sullenly.

'Me, put a spanner in the works?' Jenna affected
a light laugh while she held on to her temper—with
difficulty. 'Correct me if I'm wrong, brother dear,
but I was under the impression that the sale of your
share was already settled—that Adam is buying it in
two months.'

'But Drew will buy it now!' Clare burst in triumphantly, as if Jenna had overlooked this remarkably wonderful point.

'Over my dead body!' Jenna returned furiously. 'I'm not going to have Drew Merrick for a partner. And I won't let you back out of our agreement, Chris.'

'You can't stop me, sister dear,' Chris smiled scathingly, then switched back to his scowl. 'What's the difference who buys me out? For heaven's sake, Jenna, be reasonable. Clare and I want out, and you can't blame us for taking the first available exit, particularly since . . .'

'Yes?' Jenna's voice shook with fury.

Chris gave a surly shrug and didn't go on.

'Two months. That's all you have to wait. Two lousy months until Adam and I are married,' Jenna heard herself protesting, pleading almost.

Clare gave one of her silly, nervous giggles. 'That's just it, Jenna. Anything can happen in two months, can't it?'

Jenna stared at her in incomprehension. Clare giggled again.

Jenna stood up. 'You haven't accepted Drew's offer yet, have you?'

Chris shook his head. 'No, but . . .'

'Then hold him off, Chris. Give me time. Give me just a few days and I'll get the money somehow,' Jenna promised urgently, wildly, and stayed awake half the night trying to work out how she could foil Drew Merrick.

She knew now why he had come back—to make

trouble between herself and Adam. Paranoic? A little, perhaps, but why else had Drew turned up on the island a week before she and Adam were to formalise their relationship? And what better way to jam a wedge between them than by popping up as her business partner? Adam would have a fit; the Nashes would fall about in horror; the island would be agog, rumours flying.

There was only one way out: Adam would have to buy Chris out without waiting until the wedding; he couldn't afford the luxury of holding on to his insurance that the marriage would go through—this time.

They had been engaged once before—three years ago—when Jenna had been nineteen. It was a year after she had turned down Drew Merrick, and six months after news had reached the island that Drew had married someone in Sydney. Only, unlike Drew, Jenna had not been able to bring herself to marry on the rebound, and had broken off the engagement to Adam shortly before the wedding.

Humiliated and hurt, Adam had left for mainland Australia, but, when he returned two years later to run the island's fifteen-bed hospital, they had taken up again—out of loneliness perhaps, habit, or simply convenience. Adam had bided his time—cunningly, Jenna would have said had it been any other man than Adam. They had been going together just on a year when he proposed again last week and she had accepted, with relief as much as anything else.

Jenna tried not to think too much about deep-lying motives. Yes, she had to admit it was a convenient solution to everybody's problems, but she was very fond of Adam, and surely that was as good a basis for marriage as any violent passion—the sort of feeling she had had towards Drew? And, whatever Clare and Chris thought, she had no intention of backing out this time; the engagement would go through. And so would the wedding—her grandmother's dearest wish come true, Jenna thought sourly, and she was almost glad Sarah Anderson wasn't going to be around for the long-awaited occasion—the joining of the island's two oldest families.

Her grandmother had a lot to answer for. Jenna might have risen to the old lady's defence, hackles on end, when Drew had attacked her so callously, but he had been right; her grandmother had been a nasty old tyrant. She had prevented Jenna marrying Drew and, in her heart, Jenna could not forgive her for that—nor herself for not standing up to her. Nor Drew, for not forcing her to marry him. Somehow. He could have done, if he'd really wanted to.

Why hadn't he? Jenna had asked herself that question a thousand times over the last four years. Why had Drew taken her at her word and walked out of her life? Until she heard of his marriage, Jenna had clung on to the hope that he would come back to give her a second chance. When he didn't, when he went off and got married, it was she who felt rejected and abandoned—irrationally, since it was she who had rejected him. But Drew should have known better, should have known she was young and gullible and had been taken in by old Sarah Anderson.

Jenna had been going on eighteen, little more than a child when Drew had returned to the island on one of his rare business visits since his father's death several years earlier. The previous time he had come Jenna had been fifteen and the crush she had always had on him burgeoned into a wild infatuation. Drew had been nice to her when he came across her—suspiciously often—as nice as a young man in his twenties was likely to be towards a fifteen-year-old kid. But three years later, Jenna had blossomed into the island beauty and had the few available males angling after her—Adam Nash, fresh from medical school in Sydney, at the fore. Jenna wasn't interested in any of them; she was waiting for Drew Merrick's next visit, convinced that this time he would fall madly in love with her, a heart-warming adolescent fantasy, which in the best of fairy-tale tradition came true.

Drew *had* fallen in love with her and, a few days before he was due to fly back to Sydney, asked her to marry him. Jenna said yes, and then they made the mistake of approaching her grandmother for consent, since Jenna wasn't of age.

'A grocer's son marry my granddaughter? Over my dead body!' the old lady had hissed at Drew, the fact that Drew had already made his mark as a successful businessman not rating a bean in her grandmother's book.

'Don't tempt me,' had been Drew's sarcastic rejoinder. Jenna had been devastated, but Drew didn't seem particularly put out.

'I should have expected that,' he laughed. 'But it's all right, darling, you'll be eighteen in six weeks—legally an adult and free to marry anyone you choose—even a grocer's son, without the old tartar's consent. I'll come back for you in six weeks.

And he did. Only, in the intervening six weeks, her grandmother had taken to her bed, ill, and Jenna was torn between her love for Drew and the old lady's need of her.

'She's putting it on, Jenna, can't you see that? This is her way of keeping you from marrying me. She's no more sick than you are—than I am. Believe me, darling, she'll come round if only you stand up to her.' Drew had been furious, but there had been a sort of desperation about him, too.

One minute Jenna did believe him, the next she was riddled with guilt and duty, and in utter confusion. Drew's plan was that they left for Sydney together and married there, but until the very last moment Jenna had no idea what she was going to do.

They went out to dinner the night before they were scheduled to leave the island, and later drove to one of the deserted coves a few miles beyond Sarah Anderson's house. Jenna had been silent, scared and excited, sensing what Drew had in mind.

He made love to her on a rug spread on the grassy slope above the cove. It was a wonderful experience, if a little frightening, and afterwards, as they lay in each other's arms, Jenna truly believed that nothing, no one, could part them.

Drew had felt the same. 'Nothing can come between us now,' he had told her, and a long time later, Jenna realised that he had banked on the belief that a girl of her strict upbringing would have to marry the man who had taken her virginity. She had believed that too, yet the next morning she stayed in her room crying, as the plane she was to have been on flew over the house and out to sea, taking Drew back to Sydney without her. He had not even come to the house to argue it out with her one more time.

True to Drew's cynical prediction, her grandmother was off her sick-bed in a matter of days, as spritely as ever. Jenna was shattered. She wanted to fly to Drew immediately, but pride stopped her. So she remained on the island, trapped into being her grandmother's reluctant companion, and hoping against hope for Drew's return, until news of his marriage killed the last faint hope. It killed something in Jenna, too, as well as her love for him.

Well, he was back now, four years later and with a score to settle. Drew had shrugged off Sarah Anderson's insults, but Jenna knew he would never shrug off her own last-minute capitulation. That would have been a greater blow to his ego than anything her grandmother could have dished up, and it was no coincidence that Drew had chosen to return to the island just at the time his presence could do the most damage to her future.

CHAPTER FOUR

' AREN'T you going to the Nashes' for lunch today?'
Clare asked, coming into the kitchen late the next
morning and finding Jenna standing at the sink in
her tatty dressing-robe.

Jenna spun round, sloshing some water out of the
glass in her hand.

'Sorry, I didn't mean to startle you,' Clare apolo-
gised.

Jenna stared at her, aghast. 'I forgot,' she
breathed out in a horrified whisper. 'I completely
forgot.'

Clare looked incredulous, and Jenna didn't blame
her. She had been going to the Nashes' for Sunday
lunch every second Sunday for what seemed like a
lifetime. Today, even after Adam's reminder
yesterday, she had simply forgotten, and she was as
amazed as Clare. 'I'd better telephone Adam before
he sets off to pick me up. I can't go. Not today. My
head feels foul and I've just taken a couple of
Disprins,' Jenna explained defensively, and
wondered why she was explaining herself so hard to
her sister-in-law.

'He won't be very pleased,' Clare said primly.
'We're off now. To Judy's,' she added
unnecessarily, since they always went to Clare's
sister's place on Sunday. Sometimes, on what Jenna

termed 'non-Nash' Sundays, she went with them herself.

But this was a Nash Sunday, and how it could have slipped her mind was beyond Jenna's comprehension. When Adam answered the phone, she played up her headache for all it was worth, and then some.

'You might have let me know earlier. I was just about to leave to pick you up,' Adam rebuked her testily.

'I know. I'm sorry. But I put off telephoning until the very last moment because I thought my head might ease up enough to let me come,' Jenna lied shamelessly, and wondered what Adam would have made of her lapse of memory. The psychiatrist in him would have had a field day.

'Mother will be disappointed.' Adam sounded aggrieved, and very like his own mother.

'I know. I'm terribly sorry. Please apologise to her for me,' Jenna replied hypocritically, since she could not have cared less what Mrs Nash was going to feel. Agnes Nash was not one of her favourite people, and vice-versa. Adam's mother had not forgiven Jenna for reneging on the marriage the first time round, and was not overjoyed at the latest turn of events. Jennifer Anderson might be an Anderson, but she did not deserve Dr Adam Nash. There, Jenna had to agree with her.

'Well, take a couple of Disprins and go back to bed.' Adam slipped into his Dr Nash mode. Jenna clamped her teeth together on the other end of the line. 'We're going to have to do something about those headaches of yours, Jenna. You've been getting too many of them too often.'

Yes, Doctor, Jenna mouthed at the window with a grimace. She said, 'You mustn't worry, Adam, I'll be fine. And Adam, I need to talk to you. It's rather important. Can we have lunch soon?'

'Yes, all right,' Adam agreed grudgingly, without asking what it was she needed to talk to him about so urgently.

Jenna hung up feeling guilty, and then relieved. Then guilty again, because she felt relieved to have escaped a dreary Nash Sunday. How was she ever going to stand years of them? A lifetime? Perhaps she could persuade Adam to transfer to Sydney. Perhaps pigs might fly! Adam's life was here on this island. And so was hers.

After her bath, Jenna dressed in an old pair of jeans and an equally ancient jumper, and took herself for a long, hard walk. The beach beneath the house was not favoured by the tourists, even in the summer, nor by the islanders in any season. It was very rocky and the waves broke too unevenly and dangerously over hidden rocks for swimming, or even fishing, to be safe, and Jenna invariably had the place to herself.

She spent two moody hours by the water, trying to come up with some sort of alternative plan, just in case. Just in case Adam dug his heels in and refused to buy Chris out before the wedding. But he wouldn't do that. Jenna reassured herself one moment, and the next she was beset by every doubt in the world—about Adam and herself. In the end, she started back to the house in a worse frame than when she had left it.

She returned the long way round, along the road instead of clambering up the steep slope that led to the back of the house, and she was turning into the drive, glowering her mandatory scowl at the ever-offensive Grandma's Kitchen sign, when the toot of a horn made her jump and spin around. As the car swung into the drive, Jenna took an alarmed, unthinking step backwards, stumbled, and came down heavily in an ungainly heap on to the gravel, one ankle twisted under the weight of her body. The pain seared like a knife, and she yelped, involuntary tears springing to her eyes and spilling down her cheeks.

Drew was out of the car and at her side before she had time to think of trying to stand up. Jenna turned on him savagely. 'Of all the stupid things! Why the hell did you have to toot the horn like that?'

'I'm sorry. I was right behind you and I tooted so you wouldn't get a fright. Are you all right? Can you stand?' Drew demanded in breathless concern.

'Well, I did get a fright. And I don't know. Damn it, it hurts.' The last bit came out as a whimper. Jenna turned her face angrily away as the wretched tears kept spilling down her cheeks.

'Come on, let's get you inside,' Drew said gently, bending over her and putting an arm around her waist to ease her to her feet.

Jenna gritted her teeth to stop a whimper. The pain wasn't sharp any more, but hot and throbby. Gingerly, and with Drew's arm supporting her, she tested out the left foot; the moment it touched ground, she sprang it up again. 'You'll have to help me hobble in,' she muttered, since there was no way, save perhaps by crawling, that she was going to get herself into the house unaided.

'I've a better idea.' Drew scooped her up into his arms as if she had been Jodie, and the thing about someone scooping you up like that is that your first instinct is to fling your arms around their neck and clutch for dear life. To her chagrin, Jenna found herself clutching Drew's neck in those first startled moments pretty much as her little niece would have done. Embarrassed, she yanked one arm away and lowered the other around Drew's shoulder, barely touching the navy cashmere that covered the hard muscle underneath.

'Hang on properly, for heaven's sake,' Drew ordered, and Jenna tightened her grip a little as he carried her up the slope of the drive.

'I could have walked. With a bit of help,' she muttered sullenly. 'There's no need for this Galahad act. You'd better go around to the back door,' she added as Drew seemed about to carry her up the steps to the front door.

'Keeping me in my place?' Drew shot back with a sarcastic laugh.

'Don't be absurd! The front door is locked, the back isn't,' Jenna told him with a snap, then stayed silent, thinking that of all the back-handed ironies, this had to take the cake—Drew Merrick carrying her bodily into Sarah Anderson's house. Her grandmother would be spinning in her grave!

'Put me down now,' she ordered ungraciously when Drew had carried her into the kitchen.

He sat her down on the nearest chair and, squatting down in front of her, began to untie the laces of her sneaker. 'Leave it. I can manage that,' Jenna protested, yelping an involuntary 'Ouch!' as Drew ignored her and eased her foot out of the shoe. Then, pushing up the leg of the jeans, he carefully peeled off the sock, which to Jenna's mortification was sporting an enormous hole at the toes. Drew ran his fingers lightly over her ankle. There was no sign of any swelling, and the throbbing was already beginning to subside. The new tingling sensation had nothing to do with the ankle; it was the unnerving effect of Drew's fingers sensuously skimming over her bare skin. Jenna was appalled at her own reaction. She bit hard into her lower lip and stared silently into the top of Drew's dark head, and when he suddenly jerked his head up she was caught by surprise, with no time to turn her eyes away to slip a mask over her features. Their eyes met and locked: Drew's steady, unreadable, her own, Jenna feared, transparently tell-tale of every startling thought inside her head. Blushing and flustered, she swung her face away.

'You'll live,' Drew told her drily, springing lightly to his feet. 'I'll get a basin of cold water and you can give it a bit of a soak before I strap a bandage around it.'

'There's no need for that,' Jenna began another surly protest.

Drew raised a mocking eyebrow. 'Would you

prefer I telephone Dr Nash to come and do it for you instead?' he asked with a fatuous solicitousness that made Jenna burst out with a sound of exasperation.

'Is that a "no"?' Drew laughed, and went over to the cupboard under the sink.

'Left door; the large plastic basin,' Jenna directed, giving in with bad grace, and adding resignedly, 'The first-aid kit is in the bathroom across the hall—if you must insist on playing Dr Kildare on the heels of Sir Galahad.'

He left her sitting there with her foot in the basin of water, and went out to get the bandage, Jenna supposed, until the noises up on the roof a few moments later made her realise Drew was up there inspecting Mitchell's mens' temporary repairs which she had forgotten all about. Distracted by the fall, she had also forgotten to ask what Drew was doing here on a Sunday afternoon, anyway. Jenna readied herself for the fight they were about to have the moment Drew walked back in: about Mitchell, the roof, Drew's offer to Chris.

'I thought this was one of your duty Sundays *chez* Nash,' Drew remarked, strolling back in with a roll of bandage in his hand and deflecting Jenna from her attack.

'You really must be hard up for local gossip if you've had to resort to finding out where people eat their lunch these days,' Jenna retorted, more than a little surprised that Drew was acquainted with such trivial details of her boring life. She glowered down at him as he dropped down to her feet again and began to deftly bandage up the ankle.

Drew tossed up a grin. 'You should know that in a place like this even a change from roast beef to roast lamb almost rates a snippet in the gossip columns.'

That summed up the claustrophobic busybodiness of the island so neatly, Jenna nearly laughed. She smiled in spite of herself.

'There, that should do it.' Drew finished with the bandage. 'Now, stand up carefully and see how it feels when you put some weight on it.' Drew stood up himself, keeping a firm grip on her arm as Jenna tested out her injured foot. A twinge, that was all. The ankle felt firm and comfortable in its white strapping, and in an hour or two it would be perfectly all right again.

'It's fine. Thank you, Doctor,' she said sarcastically, with an exaggerated smile of gratitude.

Drew looked back at her for a moment with something like anger in his eyes. His return smile, when it finally came, was as malicious as the silky-smooth voice. 'Haven't you got your lovers a little mixed up?' he jeered softly.

The wave of heat in her cheeks must have turned her face beetroot. 'Very funny,' Jenna muttered, giving her arm an angry jerk to dislodge Drew's hand from it.

Drew released his grip. 'Don't go falling over in indignation now, will you?' he cautioned drily. 'Sit down again and I'll make you a cup of coffee, shall I? I could do with one myself,' he added, moving to the bench and reaching for the coffee beans without so much as waiting for her answer.

Jenna sat down. 'What are you doing here, Drew?'

He tossed her a questioning look over his shoulder as he flicked on the coffee grinder, and Jenna had to wait until he flicked it off again.

'Here. Today. What . . .' she recommenced loudly, even though the grinder had stopped.

Drew turned to her. 'There's no need to shout, I haven't gone deaf. I came by to drop off Jodie's presents. You might remember, I bought her the doll.'

'And the train-set,' Jenna put in grimly. 'Don't forget the train-set.'

'That's right. And the train-set.' Drew agreed carelessly, and returned his attention to the coffee.

Jenna waited until he had put the percolator on, then gave an angry laugh. 'You're wasting your time, Drew. It won't work.'

Lips pursed, brows together in a faint frown, Drew presented a study in puzzlement. 'Why am I wasting my time, Jenna, and what is it that won't work?' he asked, all innocent interest.

'Hah! Don't bother playing dumb with me, Drew Merrick. You know perfectly well what I mean,' Jenna retorted heatedly, but spelt it out for him anyway. 'You're wasting your time buttering up Clare with your presents for Jodie, because all the presents in the world are not going to help you get your hands on Chris's share of this restaurant, let alone this house. My home. And you had no right even to try to con it out of him behind my back,' she raged at him, her temper hanging by a thread.

'Con it out of him?' Drew repeated her phrase with distaste. 'That is not the way I do business,

Jenna. And I certainly was not going behind your back. On the contrary, I suggested to Chris that he talk it over with you first. I assume that he has.'

'Oh, yes!' Jenna's hollow laugh was almost a cackle. Talk it over with her, indeed. Some talk! If it hadn't been for Clare's—and Jessica Fenwick's—slips, she would not have been any the wiser until Chris had sold her right down the drain.

'Well, then,' said Drew, primly, as if he had made his point and was absolved from everything.

'Well, then, nothing!' Jenna snapped furiously. 'You're too late, Drew. It has all been arranged. Adam is going to buy Chris out.'

'Is he really?' Drew's eyebrow shot up. 'Then why wait until after the wedding, if he's so keen to join the ranks of businessmen, might I ask?'

He might ask, but Jenna had no intention of telling him something she only suspected and didn't want to think too much about. 'It's not your business,' she mumbled indistinctly.

Drew took in her discomfort and seemed to enjoy it. 'True. And I'm sure Dr Nash has his reasons,' he conceded politely. 'Only, in view of his curious reluctance to settle the matter, I don't think you should blame your brother for subscribing to the philosophy of a bird in the hand,' he pointed out, very reasonably. 'It also seems to me,' he continued with a wry smile, 'that given your Adam's evident reluctance to "go into trade"—is that the term?—I might even be doing him a favour by getting Chris out of your hair.'

The suggestion was preposterous. Drew Merrick

was not out to do anybody any favours, and certainly not Adam Nash. Jenna studied him with dislike. 'Who are you trying to kid, Drew? All you're after is to make trouble between me and Adam.'

'And why should I want to do that?' Drew enquired, very evenly, holding Jenna's angry eyes in a long stare.

'To pay me back, why else?' Jenna muttered harshly.

There was the slightest pause before Drew reacted with a snort of a laugh. 'If you mean what I think you mean, Jenna, then you're having yourself on. I have not been carrying a grudge against an eighteen-year-old kid who was too conditioned by her snob of a grandmother to run off with the local grocer's son.'

Jenna felt the blood leave her face as Drew's awful accusation sank in. 'But it wasn't like that! It wasn't!' The passionate denial burst out of her before she could stop it.

'Wasn't it?' Drew challenged with a bitterness that quite frightened her.

'No, it wasn't. I . . . I just changed my mind about going away with you, marrying you. That's all.' It sounded feeble and untrue.

'So you did,' agreed Drew lightly, as if the subject bored him, and he set about pouring coffee. Jenna stayed silent, torn between trying to explain how she had been trapped by her grandmother, and a dread of giving away the anguish and despair she had felt when Drew had not come back for her. If Drew wanted revenge, he had already had it. Four years of it.

'Anyway, it looks as if you and I will be in partnership yet.' Drew placed a mug of coffee in front of her.

Jenna ignored it. 'Not if I can help it,' she promised grimly, pushing out the thoughts of the past and what might have been, and bringing herself back to the here-and-now, where Drew Merrick no longer had a place.

'And you won't need to marry Adam Nash, after all,' Drew went on as if she hadn't interrupted, his eyes fixed on her face as it went blank, then showed a slow, frowning comprehension. 'That should be a load off your mind, shouldn't it? Because when it comes to the crunch, wouldn't you rather have me as a partner than Adam Nash as a husband?' Drew returned to the bench and picked up his coffee.

Jenna found her voice, high and quivering. 'Are you suggesting I'm going to marry Adam because of Chris and the restaurant? For money?' she demanded scathingly.

Drew took an unhurried sip, then lowered the cup. 'Aren't you?' he taunted, with a flickering smile that didn't reach his eyes; they were a hard, cold blue, and Jenna thought she read contempt in them. It made her feel momentarily, irrationally, mortified, and she dropped her eyes guiltily. Then, annoyed at herself for reacting in a way that was tantamount to an admission of Drew's insinuation, she jerked them back to his face.

'That's the sort of horrid insinuation I would have

expected from you,' she rallied, trying for scorn but her voice came out too unsteadily for it to have much impact; she sounded more fearful than anything else.

'Then I'm glad I haven't disappointed you,' Drew smiled with malice. 'But you haven't answered my question.'

'That's because it doesn't deserve an answer!' Jenna's outrage caught up with her at last, and she was glad to feel the rush of red-hot anger. 'How dare you imply that I'm out for what I can get—that I'd let myself use Adam?' She glared so hard, her eyes felt as though they were on stalks.

Drew was shaking his head, almost pityingly. 'Wrong. I was not implying that at all. You've never been one for using people, Jenna, it isn't in you.' His mouth tilted in wry amusement at her puzzlement at being handed an unexpected compliment.

But Jenna wasn't thick; she waited for the punchline and wasn't disappointed.

'You're the bunny who lets herself be used, Jenna, by your grandmother, your brother . . .'

'What?'

'Adam Nash . . .'

'What?' she barked again.

'You heard,' Drew said curtly. 'Your grandmother clung to you like a leech to her dying day; your brother conned you into this restaurant venture because it suited him, only now, at the first hint of a setback he wants to cut and run, so you've been elected the sacrificial lamb. Or, to put it another way, you have to sell yourself to Adam Nash so that your brother can go on to his next haywire scheme.'

Jenna's face had gone so rigid, it felt like granite, only her eyes blazed her fury at him as she listened, just waiting for him to drag Adam into it before letting fly.

'And Adam Nash is using you,' Drew continued, unperturbed by her silent rage, 'or rather, using the opportunity to get you to marry him at long last, because he knows buying you by way of bailing Chris out is the only way he's ever going to get you.'

That's what Jenna had been waiting for; the ultimate insult. 'That's what you think!' she hissed. 'I suppose it hasn't occurred to you that I might just possibly love Adam and want to marry him?'

'Frankly, no.'

'Hah! Of course not!' Jenna was out of her chair in a whirl of frenzied anger. 'You're too much of an egomaniac for that even to cross your mind.'

'Do mind your ankle,' Drew murmured sarcastically as Jenna took another agitated step towards him.

'You can't possibly imagine me being interested in any other man after you, can you? You think that just because I didn't marry you when you asked, I've been sitting around for the last four years, hoping you'll come back and give me another chance,' Jenna sneered, blocking her mind to how perilously close her taunt was to the truth.

'And haven't you?' Drew put his cup down and eased himself away from the bench, and Jenna took an instinctive, unsteady step back, suddenly aware of a shift in Drew's attitude; it was all at once loaded with menace.

Her alarm seemed to amuse Drew. He came across the room, lithe and smiling. 'What's the matter, Jenna? Afraid I'm going to put the truth to the test?' he asked softly.

'I'm not afraid of you.' The shakiness in her voice didn't back up the words. 'Don't you dare touch me! Don't!' Jenna started in real fright as Drew took one more step, closing his arms around her waist and pulling her against himself almost in the same movement. The hard, intimate contact of their bodies sent a tremor of shock through her, and made Jenna catch her breath in a sharp, indrawn gasp that brought a slow curve of malicious satisfaction to Drew's lips. He stared into her eyes while he slid his hands with sensuous pressure over the roundness of her hips, pressing her hard to himself and watching the panic rush into her eyes.

Jenna pushed frantically against his chest with both hands. 'Don't be silly, Drew,' she admonished in a misguided attempt to play it light, and then let out another sharp gasp as Drew deliberately increased the pressure of his hands on her hips.

'Let me go. Please,' Jenna pleaded in a ragged whisper. 'My foot is hurting me,' she added in belated inspiration, lying through her teeth because she couldn't feel anything but the closeness of Drew's body and her own frightening response to it. If someone had come along at that moment and chopped off her foot, it was a moot point as to whether she would even have noticed!

Drew grinned viciously. 'Nice try, Jenna,' he murmured into her lips as he brought his mouth swiftly over hers, smothering the start of her next bleat of protest, and forcing her lips apart to receive his kiss.

Later, to her humiliation, Jenna was to recall how very little pressure Drew's mouth had needed to exert to elicit her response; the mere touch of his lips seemed to have been enough to unleash the longing that had been lying dormant inside her since the night he had made love to her.

There was an instant of passive shock, no more than a split-second, and another when her reason sent its faint, frantic warning, before Jenna closed off mind and reason and abandoned herself to the surge of desire, slackening meltingly against him, her hands winding around the back of his black head while her mouth urged feverishly for appeasement of the unsatisfied ache that spanned four years.

It was a bruising, savage kiss, mindless and won-derful, and Jenna regretted every long, passionate second of it the instant their mouths broke apart. She tore her hands away from Drew's head as if his hair had suddenly caught fire, and tried to thrust him away from her, every ounce of passion turned into humiliated hate for his having proved her vul-nerability so easily. And she made it so easy for him; she had not even had the pride to put up a token struggle!

'Well, Jenna, what do you say now?' Drew's smile was positively feline. 'How long is it since you've been kissed like that?'

He knew. Four years. 'Let me go, please,' Jenna pleaded miserably, searingly conscious of the warmth of his hands still at her back. A morsel of belated pride prevented her from resorting to a hollow, indignant demand that he get them off her, or else. Or else what? She had no weapon against him. If Drew chose to kiss her again, she would respond. Again. Jenna knew that. Did Drew?

Yes, he knew. She could read the knowledge in his eyes; they were full of his triumph. Then, abruptly, Drew dropped his hands, but he didn't move away. With the table behind her making it impossible to step back from him, Jenna was virtually holding her breath in the effort to keep their bodies from touching.

Drew flicked an amused glance down at the non-existent gap between them and up to her face again. 'Why don't you sit down and rest your ankle,' he suggested tartly, and, moving away from her at last, returned to his position at the bench. Leaning back against it, he studied her in speculative silence as Jenna remained on her feet.

She was aware of the ankle emitting a faint throb, but she wanted to be ready to bolt for it if Drew so much as looked as if he was about to make another move towards her. Dull reason told her he wouldn't; he had proved what he had set out to prove. And what a boost to his ego; four years on and she was still putty in his hands, as vulnerable to him as ever she had been at eighteen! Physically. *Only* physically, Jenna told herself shakily, nothing more. She did not know this man any more—this tall, very attractive stranger who had walked into her life with the sole intention of disrupting it.

They were staring at each other now as if they were strangers sizing each other up at some party, each perhaps thinking the other looked vaguely familiar, reminding them of someone they had known. Drew broke the mutual staring by suddenly turning to the window and leaning over the sink to look down the drive. After a moment he drew away and ambled over to the side door, a curiously pleased smile on his face. Jenna heard the crunch of footsteps and then saw Adam walking past the window.

CHAPTER FIVE

'ENTER the hero. Aren't you lucky his timing is off?' Drew threw the aside at Jenna with a mean grin as he swung the door open with an abrupt flourish, to reveal Adam standing on the doorstep looking startled and a little stupid, with one hand curled into a fist and raised ready to give his 'special' knock which always got on Jenna's nerves.

'Hello, Nash, did I startle you?' Drew drawled, using his advantage maliciously. 'Sorry about my car blocking the drive. Bit of a hike from the road, isn't it? Come in, won't you?' he invited with an effusive hospitality that disconcerted Adam even more than having the door suddenly flung open in his face. 'Jenna and I were just talking about you, weren't we, Jenna?' Drew tossed her a mean flash of teeth as Jenna stood by the table, looking as much a trapped rabbit as Adam.

But Adam had been brought up in the school of Agnes Nash and Sarah Anderson, where breeding will out, and recovered his poise commendably, if a little belatedly. 'Merrick.' He gave a curt nod of reluctant acknowledgement that must have cost him a lot, given that he probably would have liked to punch Drew in his grinning face, and walked past him without another glance.

'Hello, darling.' He came up to Jenna and kissed

77

her on the mouth, resting both hands on her shoulders in a display of patently intimate affection that made Jenna blush madly. 'I was concerned about your headache and . . .'

'A headache? As well as a sprained ankle?' Drew gave a performance of startled dismay. 'You really must take better care of her, Nash,' he admonished primly. As Adam mechanically dropped his eyes to her feet, he continued, 'I bandaged it as best I could, but no doubt you'll want to rebandage it—professionally.'

'For heavens' sake!' Jenna snapped irritably. 'Drew was just leaving. Oh, don't fuss, Adam, please,' she snapped at him too, as Adam tried to ease her to the chair.

'Yes, I've been trying to get her to sit down, too.' Drew nodded approvingly. 'But she will insist on standing. Then, of course, you're allowed to be firm with her, since I gather you two have become engaged. Again. My congratulations, Nash.'

Drew was being preposterous and was enjoying himself to his back teeth. Jenna wanted to pick up something and throw it at him; Adam was a sullen, glowering red that rather unfortunately matched the burgundy tie around his neck. Nash Sundays were dressy affairs, and Adam was in a dark suit and white shirt, looking very stiff and formal beside Drew's understated sports wear and Jenna's own scruffy casualness. Embarrassed into slow-wittedness, neither of them could think of a thing to say in the face of Drew's outrageousness.

Drew carried on, blithely. 'Incidentally, Nash, I

don't think Jenna has had a chance to tell you yet that I'm arranging to buy her brother out, has she?' He changed tack only to score another point off the hapless Adam.

Adam darted Jenna a blank look.

'That's not true!' Jenna contradicted furiously. 'He's only made Chris an offer, and we . . . Chris hasn't accepted it yet. He isn't going to, either,' she added defiantly.

Adam seemed to make an effort to draw himself up to his full height, which, at five foot nine, was only two inches taller than Jenna, and short of Drew's six-foot-plus by a good few inches. He looked at Drew with cold dislike. 'Stay out of our business, Merrick.'

'Ah, but I'm always interested in business, you know that,' Drew returned, infuriatingly pleasant, and Jenna could feel Adam going positively rigid beside her. If she had glanced down she knew she would have seen his fists clenching and unclenching at his sides in impotent anger.

Drew made a show of examining his watch. 'Dear me, is that the time? I'm afraid I must leave you,' he smiled regretfully. 'All right if I just leave Jodie's presents on the veranda, Jenna? It would save me coming in again.'

Her teeth would be ground to the gums in repressed fury if he didn't get out of the place in the next few seconds, and she wouldn't be responsible for her actions if Drew dared to come again.

'Oh, I almost forgot.' Drew turned from the door, dragging every ounce of frustration out of his exit.

'I'm having a dinner tomorrow night at my hotel—the Bayview,' he reminded them, as if they were likely to have forgotten that Drew owned the best hotel on the island. 'And since you're going to have to be closed here for the next week or so, I hope you'll be able to come, Jenna. You too, of course, Nash.' Drew included Adam in his gratuitous invitation with gushing courtesy.

'Giving yourself a welcome-home party because no one else is putting one on for you?' Jenna couldn't help taunting.

Drew grinned, not the least put out. 'Something like that,' he agreed cheerfully, and let himself out at last, whistling as he went. His whistle floated back to them from the path, and then faded away as Drew rounded the curve of the drive.

Adam's face was so rigid it could have cracked; his eyes were brown wells of suspicion under the sandy brows.

'And what was all that about?' The harshness came grating out through his compressed lips.

Jenna sat down wearily, wishing he would go away, too, and leave her alone. 'Drew was just being annoying. Nothing has been settled with Chris. Why don't you pour yourself a coffee and sit down?' she suggested soothingly as he hovered edgily in front of her.

'What was he doing here in the first place, that's what I want to know? And what happened to your ankle?' Adam stared down at her accusingly, unplacated.

Jenna gritted her teeth. 'He came to bring Jodie's

birthday present, and I happened to trip on the drive just as he turned up. I'd been down to the beach to try and clear the headache,' she explained, patiently, giving the bare bones of the truth, and saw the suspicion begin to fade out of Adam's eyes as he accepted the facile explanation—because he needed to. Jenna wondered what he would say if she had added, and he carried me into the house, bandaged my ankle and then we had a mad, passionate kiss that I suspect has rather turned my world upside-down if I had a moment to think about it!

Adam gave a grunt. 'He was behaving like an idiot.'

'Yes.' Hell-bent on making trouble between her and Adam—and succeeding, if this uptight edginess left in his wake was any measure. 'Adam,' Jenna appealed suddenly, 'about buying Chris out . . .' she faltered as his face went all pinched and tight again, then continued with a brightness that rang so hollow, it was awful. 'Well, I was thinking . . . what with Clare pregnant, and Chris being so anxious and pressed for money, could we . . . couldn't you . . . well . . .' She was making a incoherent hash of it. Jenna began again. 'Look, I know we agreed that you'd buy Chris out after we got married, but couldn't you do it early? Now? It would make everything so much more settled, wouldn't it? Please, Adam.' Her appeal sounded faintly desperate.

Adam wandered moodily over to the window and then back to the table again—all without a word.

'I don't want Drew Merrick as a business partner, Adam. And if Chris gives in—Clare is all for it, and egging him on—then . . . You can't want that to happen, Adam.'

Adam was studying her with a curious expression: curious for him, faintly cynical, and if Jenna didn't know him better she would have said, with malice; a word she wouldn't have dreamt of applying to him. To Drew, yes, never Adam.

'Perhaps it's not such a bad idea to let him have it.'

Jenna stared at him, incredulous.

Adam went on, 'And for you to sell your share to him as well. Let him have the whole place, restaurant and house if he wants it. We don't need it, Jenna.' Adam's voice took on an authoritative edge—the sort of voice Jenna assumed he used with his patients. 'You must know I would prefer you not to be involved in any sort of business after we're married. I'm not saying you couldn't make this restaurant a success. If anyone could, you could,' he added in what sounded like downright flattery, 'only after we're married you won't have time for it, Jenna. There'll be other things that will have to take priority. You must know that.'

Jenna knew, being Dr Nash's wife, mother to his children, running the hospital auxiliary, being a pillar of the island's 'society'. Oh, she knew all right, and in accepting Adam's proposal had come to terms with the predictable and the inevitable. But the restaurant had been in the background, a retention of her independence. Jenna shook her head slowly. 'It's important to me, Adam.'

They looked at each other in the uncomfortable

silence that went on for too long, then Adam shrugged. 'Well, that's it, then,' he said, decisively almost, except that it was no decision at all, and nothing had been resolved. Then he seemed not to know what to say or do next. 'Do you want me to check that ankle?' he asked brusquely, resorting to professionalism, but didn't press when Jenna gave a quick, impatient shake of her head and felt the gap widening between them.

'I'm sorry about missing lunch today. I hope your mother wasn't too put out.' She remembered to get the apology in, and wished she had been safe and sound in the midst of a dreary Sunday lunch rather than prey to Drew's unwelcome visit.

She took the bandage off after Adam left, to save herself another round of explanations when Chris and Clare returned, but had to mention Drew's visit to account for the two large, gaily wrapped boxes which she had brought inside.

'Yes, I know. We came across him in the town. On our way to Judy's.' Clare went a little pink as she came out with her lie, knowing Jenna knew it was a lie since they didn't have to go anywhere near the town to get to Judy's place.

Jenna let it pass unchallenged. Later, when she was getting ready for bed, Clare tapped on the bedroom door and came in, nervously. 'I . . . can we talk?' she asked, looking as if it was the last thing she wanted to do.

'What do you want to talk about?' Jenna returned discouragingly, and remained seated on the bed, waiting for Drew Merrick's name to pop up. She wasn't disappointed.

'I . . . when I said we came across Drew in town today, well . . . I . . . we didn't—just come across him, I mean,' Clare explained disjointedly. 'We went to see him at his hotel before going to Judy's. It was all arranged.'

She wasn't telling Jenna anything Jenna hadn't suspected.

'And I suppose you told him I hadn't gone to the Nashes?'

'Yes, I did.' Clare came away from the door and sat tentatively on the edge of the bed. 'Drew said he'd come by and drop off Jodie's presents. You didn't mind?

'As a matter of fact, I did. A lot. Was that what you wanted to tell me? I'm rather tired.'

'I want Chris to sell his share to Drew,' Clare said in a rush, meeting Jenna's eyes; she was embarrassed but curiously firm—dogged could have been the word. Jenna stared back at her sister-in-law stonily, unsurprised, but with an anger building up inside her. 'Chris is worried about upsetting you,' Clare went on when Jenna stayed silent, 'but I think we should sell to Drew rather than wait for Adam to buy him out after you two get married. That's two months away and, well, anything can happen in two months.'

Jenna smiled snakily. 'You've taken to repeating yourself, Clare; you already pointed that out to me yesterday, have you forgotten? However, since you can't seem to resist bringing up the subject, what exactly do you think is going to happen in those two months? I'm curious.'

Sarcasm always almost reduced Clare to tears; she looked tearful now, chewing away at the inside of her bottom lip, and Jenna was just starting to feel a twinge of remorse when all of a sudden Clare sprang to her feet in an ungainly jump and hurried across to the door. 'I think you're going to break off your engagement to Adam and not marry him at all! That's what I think is going to happen,' she flung at Jenna in a spiteful, triumphant little burst, and fled the room, leaving the door swinging open behind her.

It was out into the open at last. Jenna sighed wearily as she went over and closed the door.

She had a bad night, and awakened to Jodie's shrieks of delight—at Drew's presents, Jenna supposed—with a surge of sharp, if unfair, resentment towards the child as well as towards Drew.

Clare was in the kitchen, washing up after Chris's breakfast, when Jenna came in just as the telephone began to ring. 'I'll get it,' she said as Clare started reaching for a tea-towel to wipe her hands. 'Good morning, Grandma's Kitchen,' she greeted the caller ungraciously.

'If that's the way you treat your customers, I'm not surprised they're too scared to come near the place.'

Jenna counted to five in her head and managed to resist the temptation to slam the phone down in Drew's ear.

'And we really will have to do something about that name.'

'I wouldn't count my chickens, if I were you. What do you want, Drew?' At the sink, Clare's shoulders gave a little jerk at the mention of Drew's name.

'Apart from wanting to hear your bad-tempered voice, you mean?' Drew laughed tightly. 'Incidentally, will you be coming to my dinner tonight?'

Jenna grated out an angry laugh. 'Don't be stupid!'

'I'll take that as a "no", shall I?' Drew chuckled, without a dint in his irritating good humour. 'Now, before you slam the phone down on me, is your sister-in-law there, please?'

'Clare?'

'I believe that is her name, unless you've another sister-in-law tucked away somewhere.'

Clare was already turning around and wiping her hands on the tea-towel, showing no surprise that Drew should be wanting to talk to her. Jenna handed her the receiver, without a word, and started to walk out; then, changing her mind, she came back into the room. Clare gave a miffed glance.

'Yes, Drew. That will be fine, Drew. I . . . I think so.' With Jenna in ear's range, Clare was nervous and abrupt. Taking pity on her, Jenna wandered out and went to the sitting-room.

Chris had set up the train-set in the middle of the floor; beside it lay the large, expensive doll, and beside them on the floor, Jodie looked as if all her

Christmases had come at once. 'Uncle Drew . . .' She waved a tubby hand over her new possessions.

Good old uncle Drew, thought Jenna sourly, 'Nice,' she murmured, and, kneeling down on the floor, played at trains and dolls with the child until Clare came in.

'I'll be popping into town shortly,' she said, trying to sound casual and missing the mark by a long shot. 'Will you mind looking after Jodie for a while?'

Jenna got to her feet. 'Sorry, but I have to go in myself straight after breakfast.'

'Oh. Never mind, I can take her around to Judy's.' Clare tried not to sound put out.

'Planning to "come across" Drew Merrick, by any chance?' Jenna taunted. 'Tut, tut! Whatever will Chris say?' She walked past the flushing Clare, feeling mean but unrepentant, and, underneath it all, frightened sick that it was all coming to a head so quickly, that having recognised the weak link in the family chain, Drew was pulling out all stops to work on Clare. An invitation to lunch or something, more presents for Jodie coming up too, no doubt; Clare was already as good as won over.

It was funny how mousy, unassertive women like Clare could turn out so strong and stubborn at a moment's notice. Not that Jenna could really blame her for wanting to take the chance while it was offered. Drew's wretched bird in the hand was worth any number in the bush as far as Clare was concerned. She was wrong in thinking Jenna was going to back out of marrying Adam at the last

minute again—rationalisation, Jenna suspected, so
that Clare could feel better about pressuring Chris
into selling to Drew. And Chris wouldn't hold out
for long. Chris was always for the easiest way out of
anything.

Jenna didn't ring her bank manager, because it
would have been too easy for him to put her off over
the telephone, so she turned up on his doorstep
instead, or rather at his office door, and he had to see
her, appointment or not. Her grandmother's name
still counted for something with the snobs on the
island, but that something wasn't cash.

She hadn't expected Tom Boyer to beam at her
and hand over a cheque for—what? Forty, fifty
thousand dollars? And the sick feeling inside her was
not disappointment, it was just a sick feeling; but
Jenna kept her end up, keeping desperation out of
her voice as she tried to make her proposterous
request sound like a perfectly feasible business
preposition. She listened to herself quite
dispassionately, telling the po-faced man across the
desk how the restaurant would soon be out of the red
and making a profit; how she would be able not only
to service the existing loan but any new one, and
then she wondered whether she wouldn't have done
better by hurling herself at his ankles and bawling
her eyes out.

So much for the last-ditch alternative. Jenna went
home feeling humiliated, and aware that it would be
all around the island in no time that something was
amiss with the Andersons. Rumour would have it

that the Nashes had changed their minds about buying into the restaurant, or that her engagement to Adam was over before it was even officially announced. There was no such thing as privacy on the island, and there would be no end to the wild interpretations put on her unscheduled visit to the bank manager. Oh, hell, let them talk!

She beat Clare home by a couple of hours. Her sister-in-law looked guilty and vaguely defiant when she came in, and didn't volunteer a word about her appointment with Drew. Not that Jenna had expected her to. By tacit agreement, they stayed out of each other's way, Jenna taking herself off to the beach and leaving the house to Clare and the child.

Chris's car was in the drive when she returned to the house, but Chris was obviously intent on keeping out of her way, too. Coward, thought Jenna, but she wasn't in a frame of mind to face him in the sitting-room just to start another fight. Clare poked her head out of the room as Jenna was going past on her way to her own bedroom.

'You're not planning to go to Drew's dinner tonight, are you?'

Jenna fixed her with a withering look. 'What do you think? Why?' she demanded on a surly afterthought.

'Well . . . I . . . we . . . Chris and I are going.'

'Are you really? Well, that *is* a surprise!'

'And we . . . I thought perhaps you wouldn't mind baby-sitting Jodie,' Clare went on bravely, in the face of Jenna's mock astonishment. 'If you're not doing anything, that is. With Adam.'

'No, I'm not doing anything, with or without Adam, so you two can go for your fun evening—be wined and dined and make the most of it. It will be all a tax deduction for Mr Merrick, no doubt, since I can't believe he's going to entertain half the island out of the generosity of his heart.'

'Thank you,' Clare said meekly, determinedly ignoring every bit of heavy-handed sarcasm and making Jenna feel a rotter.

'I'm sorry. Go and have a nice time,' she said contritely. 'Only . . .' Clare waited for her to go on. Jenna shrugged. 'Just try to hold off signing anything away to Drew for a little longer, will you?'

Clare's soft mouth tightened into a clamp; she dropped her eyes, evasively, and Jenna's brief moment of contriteness vanished. 'Oh, do what you like!' she muttered, and went to shut herself up in her room, not emerging until Clare rapped on the door to say that they were about to leave.

'Jodie's asleep and shouldn't wake unless the wind really blows up. It's rather blustery at the moment, but Chris said we shouldn't be having another storm,' Clare reassured her anxiously. 'You will be all right, won't you?'

'Sure, I'll be fine. You look very nice,' Jenna muttered brusquely. Clare was in her 'best' maternity dress—from the last pregnancy; it was pink and pretty and smelt faintly of mothballs.

'Thank you.' Clare looked surprised and embarrassed. To receive a compliment? Was Jenna becoming such a shrew that a small pleasantry startled people out of their wits? She sighed inwardly, and felt a stab of real dislike for the upright, unpleasant person she was becoming; had become?

'Will you be all right?' Chris repeated Clare's question in a gruff mutter as Jenna was seeing them off. Her brother looked unfamiliar and ill at ease in his old dinner-suit, the formal blackness heightening his dark clolouring almost to the point of swarthiness. He avoided Jenna's eyes as much as he could, and that made him look slightly shifty as well.

Jenna smiled brightly. 'Of course I'll be all right. Have a nice time, both of you,' she added, too brightly, trying to make out she didn't care that they were off to Drew Merrick's dinner, when she *did* care—a lot.

Chris and Clare's sitting-room was the only room in the enormous house apart from her own bedroom that was half-way cosy and, after her bath, Jenna settled herself in there and put on a tape. The wind was very blustery, but it didn't sound like a storm coming. There were winds and there were winds, and Jenna's phobia made her into something of an expert when it came to distinguishing one from another, so when Adam rang about an hour later to ask whether she would like him to come over, she told him tartly it was she who was doing the baby-sitting and didn't need anyone to baby-sit her through a few gusts of wind. After she had hung up, she regretted the tartness; Adam had only been trying to be considerate and, knowing how much her fear of storms irritated him, she could at least have

thanked him for his concern—or sense of duty.
Neither of them had mentioned the island's gala
event of the night, but Adam had taken it for
granted that Chris and Clare had gone to it. Why
not? Half the island would have hot-footed it to the
dinner; the other half would be grinding their teeth
because they hadn't been invited.

Jenna was looking in on Jodie when she thought
she heard hammering. Wind rising, she told herself,
annoyed by the stupid spasm of alarm that had shot
through her willy-nilly. Then, when the sound came
again, this time more distinct and discernible, she
realised it was someone knocking at the kitchen
door. Adam. Her tartness notwithstanding, his
stolid sense of duty or concern must have got the
better of him, and he had come to keep her
company.

'I hope my knocking didn't frighten you.'

The suppressed irritation that had been for Adam
turned into a bolt of raging hostility at the sight of
Drew on the doorstep, and if she had been thinking
quickly enough, Jenna would have slammed the
door in his face. The thought came too late, and
Drew was stepping inside. 'It's turned chilly out
there with the wind. You don't mind if I come in for
a moment, do you?' he asked, already in the room
and closing the door quickly against the blast of wind
rushing into the kitchen.

'Be my guest.'

Drew ignored the dripping sarcasm. 'I thought
you might appreciate some company.' His eyes
ranged over her, and Jenna thought for a moment

that there was a flicker of something like concern in them.

'You thought wrong—as usual,' she retorted, swinging away from him and shivering a little as she pulled her robe more tightly around herself—the same tatty old robe he had caught her in before—but even without the sharp contrast of her shabbiness, Drew would have looked stunning. He was one of those men who, unlike her brother, looked born to wear formal clothes. The black which made Chris look swarthy only enhanced Drew's tanned good looks; the wind had tousled up the black curls, but even that only made his elegance more casual.

Drew ran his fingers through his hair, pushing a couple of windblown waves off his forehead. 'You're alone, I take it, apart from the child, that is?'

There was nothing in his voice that was overtly threatening, yet all at once Jenna felt something spring into a knot inside her, and she found herself wishing she had let Adam come over, after all.

She looked back blandly, hoping her nervousness wasn't showing. 'So much for the island welcome you were forced to give yourself,' Jenna jeered. As Drew's brows came together in vague puzzlement, she went on, gathering as much malice into her voice as it could hold, 'I take it that your dinner was not exactly the social coup you'd anticipated, since it seems to have fizzled out by . . . what?' Jenna brought up her wrist and examined her watch. 'Ten o'clock. Dear me, how very galling for you!' She intensified the mockery in her smile, her nervousness fading. Chris and Clare would be home

at any moment; they must have arranged to meet
Drew here for more discussions or something, and
Drew had beaten them home.

Drew smiled and said nothing.

'I do hope your girlfriend didn't find it too much
of an embarrassment.' Jenna oozed concern.

This time Drew's quick frown looked for all the
world like astonishment; then it cleared. 'Are you
talking about Jessica, by any chance?' The amused
glint in his eyes made Jenna want to kick herself;
bringing up Jessica Fenwick out of the blue like that
smacked of pure feminine curiosity.

'If you are, you'll be reassured to know that when
I left, Jessica was enjoying herself very much. I
assume she still is,' Drew told her with a trace of a
grin.

Jenna slowly added two and two, and wasn't sure
she had got the right answer. 'Do you mean to say
you walked out of your own dinner? Before it
finished?'

'Terribly rude of me, wasn't it?' Drew sounded as
if he couldn't have cared less. 'But I'm sure my
guests won't miss their host for another hour or so.
You know yourself what these island shindigs are
like when everyone gets going and a good time is
being had by all.'

The nerve-ends all came alive inside her again as
Jenna's alarm resurfaced. Drew coming here after
the dinner to talk to Chris and Clare was one thing;
leaving his own party in the middle of it was quite
another, never mind whether he was missed or not.
And Drew was playing at modesty, saying he

wouldn't be missed; everybody would be agog with curiosity about his disappearance. If it ever came out that he had left to go and call on Jennifer Anderson at this time of night, the islanders would be keeling over in thrilled horror. And if Adam found out . . .

CHAPTER SIX

'WHY have you come, Drew?' Jenna asked evenly, her eyes searching his face for an answer when Drew didn't give one.

'Any chance of a drink—other than coffee, I mean?' he asked instead, but Jenna refused to be put off.

'Answer my question, Drew. I have a right to know why you've come barging in here at this hour of the night, when you're supposed to be lording it over the natives.'

'I didn't barge in, and I haven't taken to lording it over anybody yet,' Drew mutterd testily. 'I told you when I came in that I thought you might want some company.' He turned away and, going to the door, bent down to push the draught-stopper tightly against the bottom of the door. 'I don't think the wind will come to anything much tonight,' he said and it seemed to Jenna as if he were reassuring her. When he straightened up and looked at her, the curious concern was in his eyes; this time Jenna was sure of it, and it threw her into confusion.

She stared, frowning. Drew turning up to be with her in case a storm blew up?

'What about that drink? And can't we get out of this kitchen? It's like a bloody wind-tunnel in here, with the blasts coming down the chimney.'

It *was* cold. Another shiver shot through her. Jenna gripped the lapels of her robe more tightly.

'Come on, you're freezing here.' Drew made to put an arm around her shoulder, but appeared to think better of it and took it away before he had touched her. 'Let's go into the sitting-room and I'll fix us a drink. You could probably do with one, and so could I. A night like this rather sets one's teeth on edge, doesn't it?'

Drew was being tactful, including himself in the last comment, but, tactful or no, he was taking over, just as he had done on the night of the storm. She should have resented it and put a stop to it there and then, only that unexpected air of concern—kindness almost—made Jenna hesitate. Drew was right: the wind *had* been setting her teeth on edge, and though she would have died before admitting it, she felt an enormous sense of relief just to have someone other than a sleeping child in the large house with her, even if that someone did happen to be Drew.

She hesitated a moment longer, and then lifted a shoulder in a slight shrug. 'The drinks are in the bar in the restaurant. I'll have a port,' she added, capitulating, and led the way out into the corridor, going on into the sitting-room, while Drew went off to get the drinks.

Jenna had put on a new tape, a soft, haunting melody, and she switched off the main light, turning on the heavily shaded side-lamp to minimise the shabbiness of the room. It wasn't until she saw Drew's quickly suppressed start of surprise that it dawned on her what a bad idea that had been. The room had all the tawdry overtones of a stage seduction scene. It was too late now to dart across the room and turn the main light back on, but she leant over quickly to the cassette-player and flicked it off abruptly.

'What did you do that for?' Drew asked, coming over to her side of the room with the tray of drinks and handing her her port. He had poured a very small whisky for himself, and had also ferreted out some dry biscuits which he had tossed carelessly on to the tray.

'There's no point having it on; you can't hear anything above the wind,' Jenna lied brusquely. 'Don't tell me you didn't get enough to eat at your own dinner?' she added hastily for distraction, as Drew picked up a cracker and popped it into his mouth.

'You know what these dinners are like.' Drew smiled ruefully when he had swallowed the last of his biscuit. 'Everybody talks at you so much, it's hard to get more than a couple of decent mouthfuls before the plate is whisked away from under your nose. You should have come.'

'So I could have had my plate whisked away from under my nose, too?' It wasn't a snipe; she was teasing, and was as much surprised by her own laugh as Drew. 'Do sit down,' Jenna invited awkwardly, and carrying her port with her to an armchair she sat down herself.

'Thank you,' Drew replied a shade formally, and then, setting the tray down on the coffee-table which was pushed against the wall to make room for Jodie's train-set still on the floor in the middle of the room, he skirted around the arrays of tracks and carriages and settled himself into the armchair opposite Jenna, holding his glass on his knee. He indicated the train-set with a nod. 'She does like it?' The odd note of uncertainty in his voice surprised Jenna.

'Loves it,' she assured him with a smile. 'She's been in seventh heaven ever since she clapped eyes on it.' Jenna's smile faded. 'Jodie has never had much . . . we can't . . .' She trailed off with a shrug, unable to say outright that they couldn't afford to buy toys for the child. And Drew knew that, anyway. 'She loves the doll, too.'

'I'm glad,' said Drew simply, and it sounded as if it had been important to him to know Jodie had been pleased with her presents.

She had been cruelly wrong about Drew's motives: he hadn't used Jodie to bring pressure on Clare, he had bought the child presents because he had wanted to give her pleasure. Jenna had the grace to feel an uncomfortable stab of remorse. 'It was very nice of you to get her the presents,' she mumbled by way of apology for the insulting assumption Drew didn't know she had made about him. Or did he?

Drew smiled wryly as he brought the whisky to his lips; very quickly he took it away again, but Jenna hadn't missed the small, involuntary grimace as the taste had caught him by surprise. It was rotten whisky; even at the island's duty-free prices, they could not afford anything more than the third-rate stuff that seared your throat like paint-stripper.

Jenna burst out with a laugh. 'You're allowed to

shudder if you want, I shan't be offended.'

Drew grinned sheepishly. 'I have tasted better,' he admitted with tactful understatement, and bravely took another sip. 'It's not all that bad.'

'Once your taste-buds are anaesthetised?' Jenna laughed again and sipped at her own port—no great shakes, either—and wondered if she was imagining all this: herself and Drew sitting companiably opposite each other in her grandmother's old armchairs, with a child's train-set between them as they cosily sipped drinks while the wind howled at the window. It was not like old times, because they had never done anything like this before—having had no place to sit about like an old married couple. An old married couple? What was she thinking? What was *Drew* thinking?

Jenna met his eyes in the silence. Drew looked back at her steadily, a faint smile playing around his lips. Perhaps she had it all wrong; perhaps Drew had not returned to the island to create mischief for her. Looking at him now, Jenna had the sense that, if they could talk now, everything would be all right. They could clear up all the loose ends and misunderstandings of the past. 'Drew——' she began urgently, and then jerked forward in her seat. 'What was that?'

'Wind,' Drew reassured her, and then frowned, listening.

'No, I'm sure I heard—Jodie!' Jenna leapt up and started out of the room, Drew on her heels.

Jodie had banged the kitchen door shut after herself as she wandered out into the corridor, disorientated and frightened, her little face puckered for a howl at finding herself abandoned.

'Here we are, darling.' Jenna ran towards her, but it was Drew who scooped the child up into his arms. Jodie's feet were bare on the stone floor, and her little body shivered violently inside its flannel pyjamas. Drew wrapped his arms tightly around her, hugging her close. 'Hello, young lady, ready to go back to bed now? You don't want to catch cold, do you?'

Reassured instantly and her fright forgotten, Jodie beamed with delight into Drew's face. 'Unca Drew.'

'That's right. I've come to tuck you into bed.'

Jenna led him into the child's room, a small alcove off Chris and Clare's bedroom, and Jodie allowed herself to be settled back into bed without protest, smiling sleepily up at Drew as he tucked her in.

'Train . . . doll,' she murmured, obviously making the right connection as to where her gifts had come from.

'Yes. And you liked them, didn't you?' The affection in Drew's smile was too genuine to doubt, and again Jenna mentally took back every mean thought that had crossed her mind about Drew's callously using the child for his own ends.

One moment Jodie was smiling up at him, the next she was out like a light. Leaning over, Drew gently brushed a strand of hair from her cheek. 'I wish I could fall asleep like that,' he said softly, straightening up but still gazing at the sleeping

Jodie, who looked enchantingly beautiful and as innocent as the baby she was.

Given the combination of circumstances, perhaps it wasn't all that surprising the track Jenna's thoughts were running along as she and Drew stood side by side, watching the child sleep. Crazy, but not surprising—an extension of the projection that had already started in the sitting-room. She and Drew, a married couple, watching their child sleep. And it *could* have been their child if she had had the baby she hoped so desperately Drew had given her on that one occasion they had made love; the child would have been Jodie's age now, and perhaps she and Drew . . . Crazy! Jenna tried to pull herself together. Drew hadn't given her a child and they were not married—and never likely to be.

Agitated and angry with herself, and fighting the sudden, stupid lump in her throat, Jenna made a dash out of the room, back into the sitting-room, a ridiculous choice she realised later; she would have been safer—from herself—in the kitchen, because back in the dimly lit sitting-room where all the crazy thoughts had started she was as vulnerable and unresisting as Jodie when Drew caught up with her and gathered her into his arms, holding her tightly against his chest.

Jenna could feel his warm breath in her hair as she pressed her face into his shoulder, slackening against him unthinkingly and feeling vaguely comforted and momentarily protected from that unexpected attack of pain that had reared up from nowhere and had the effect of physically winding her.

She had not felt like that for years. In the early weeks and months after Drew's departure, the corrosive feeling of pain eating away at her had always been there, tormenting her sleep and every waking moment. And then the cold, numbed hardness had set in when she heard of Drew's marriage, and that had blocked out the memories of how it had felt to be with him, seeing him smile at her, be in his arms, be kissed by him. Tonight, a crack had opened in her emotional armour and the past had slipped in, bringing with it an unbearably poignant picture of the future they had never had.

Jenna pulled her face away from Drew's shoulder and gave a scratchy laugh. 'I'm all right now. It's the storm. Wind always does that to me—you remember, I've always been an idiot about storms.' She risked a flick of an eye at his face. 'And then I got a fright when Jodie . . . oh, hell, let me go, Drew, please. I'm fine now,' Jenna lied away, wondering what other rubbish she was going to come out with, then laughed again, frightened she was going to start crying.

'Jenna, don't.' Drew put a hand under her chin and tilted her face up so that she had to look into his eyes. 'I understand,' he said softly.

Jenna shook her head. He couldn't have a clue. How could he, when he had gone away believing she had thought better of marrying him because she was an Anderson and a snob, and had returned now only to pay her back for the imagined insult? How could Drew understand what she had gone through then, was going through all over again since the night the storm had brought him back into her life?

Jenna shook her head agitatedly. 'You don't. You can't!'

'Hush.' Drew cupped her face with both hands, holding her head immobile. His lips were firm and warm as they came down to smother her protests with soft, insistent little kisses which kept intensifying in pressure, becoming harder and deeper, until in the end the agitation stilled her and her lips parted to respond. And then there was only one kiss, long and dizzyingly deep. Jenna felt she was going to swoon.

Their mouths still locked, Drew took his hands away from her face, cradling one around the back of her head and lacing his fingers sensuously through the hair; the other was slipping inside her robe, reaching into the pyjama top and sliding over bare, warm skin to close over her breast. It lay there for a moment, heavy and still, and then slowly began to move exploringly over the soft curve, as if Drew's fingers needed to reassure themselves of her familiar form, stroking, brushing the hardening nipple, gently at first, then with a gathering urgency that had Jenna arching uncontrollably.

She could barely breath when their mouths broke apart. Drew's hand stayed inside her top, his fingers carrying on with their exquisite torment while his eyes held hers, watching every nuance of arousal in her face.

Her breath was coming in whimpery little gasps. She felt exposed and vulnerable, aching, not satisfied, knowing that she must put an end to this in the next moment—or it would not end at all. And still Jenna held off. Drew's mouth was covering hers again in those soft, insistent kisses that kept her desire peaking in sharp, dizzying flares.

'Come to bed, darling,' he urged into her lips, and it was she who was cupping his face now, holding it hard to her own and kissing him as if there were no tomorrow.

'Come to bed,' Drew repeated with a mounting urgency as he pulled his mouth away; his breathing was short and ragged, and his eyes burned with a feverish reflection of her arousal. 'I want to make love to you.'

The words flashed the memory of Drew's lovemaking searingly in front of Jenna's eyes—so graphic and intense, it made her feel weak. One more time . . . just one more time, a traitorous voice pleaded inside her desire-fuddled brain. Or had she moaned it aloud?

Drew's fingers came alive at her breast again as he lowered his mouth to hers. It would have only taken that one more kiss for the last of her resistance to melt; they both knew that, and Drew's lips were already urging her capitulation when Jenna's reason came rushing back from wherever it had gone. It was like having a bucket of cold water dashed over her.

'No. Oh, no!' Jenna tore herself wildly away from Drew's mouth, from the hand that was turning her body into a pliant mass of pure sensation. Her fingers were trembling as she fumbled at the buttons of her pyjama top, but she managed to do them up and then wound the robe tightly around herself as Drew watched. The moments of insanity were over, and Jenna was shocked through and through at how close she had come to giving Drew his triumph, not to say revenge, 'Go away, Drew, you must go away. From the island. Please don't stay to mess up my life again.'

Everything about Drew changed in a flash; the last of the desire vanished from his eyes without a trace, the new light in them a savage, burning anger. 'Repeat that for me, Jenna. I'm not sure I heard you correctly. Did you mean to say *I* messed up *your* life?' The voice rasped with harshness.

Jenna took an instinctive step away from him, more than a little frightened by the sense of violence about him.

And then it was gone.

'So you think I messed up your life at some stage, and might just mess it up again?' The harshness had been replaced with sarcasm; Jenna was familiar with that and with the mockery in Drew's accompanying laugh. 'Well, that's a novel point of view, I must say. Would you care to elaborate on it?' Drew invited with poisonous politeness.

Jenna flushed and stammered. 'You . . . you know what I meant.'

Drew cocked a quizzical eyebrow.

'Yes, you did, so you needn't talk at me with your eyebrows like that,' Jenna rallied at him heatedly. 'You do know what I meant—mean. Coming back here to the island after all this time. Now—when I don't want you here, when . . .' Why was she bothering to explain, and sounding so pathetically piteous while she was about it? She gathered together the remnants of her dignity. 'I'm going to marry Adam,' she said, very firmly. 'I know you've only come back to try and spoil things for me, but it won't work, Drew. I won't let it. I don't know how you found out about Chris wanting to sell his share, and managed to time it so well to come and try to put a spoke in the wheel, but I'm telling you, it won't work.' The firmness was fading out of her voice. 'Please Drew, can't you forget what I did to you and just go away and . . .' She was appealing again, damn it!

'And let bygones be bygones?' Drew prompted with a soft sneer. 'Wish you all the best for a happy future as Mrs Nash and go on my merry way?' He gave a jarring laugh. 'I'd like to be co-operative, Jenna, but I'm afraid it's out of my hands now.'

Drew went over to the armchair he had been sitting in when Jodie had interrupted them, and picked up the unfinished drink which he had put on the floor beside the chair. He took several slow sips of the whisky without a flinch, eyeing her speculatively over the rim of the glass as Jenna remained where she was, watching him watching her, and knowing he was about to spring something on her, because that fatuous regret in his voice had to be a lead-in to something unpleasant.

Drew lowered his glass. 'You see, Jenna, now that I'm your business partner I'm going to have to keep dropping by quite regularly to check how things are going—how you're managing our joint business.'

Jenna was very slow to react; she stared, frowning,

for a long moment. 'Are you telling me that Chris . . .?' Drew's smug smile was confirmation enough. 'When?'

Drew got up without answering and, stepping around the train-set, took his glass to the tray on the coffee-table. Then he glanced at his watch and looked annoyed as he registered the time.

'When, Drew? When did Chris sell me out?' Jenna demanded furiously.

'Don't be so melodramatic, Jenna. Selling out is such an emotive term. We signed the note of sale today at lunch time. I take it that it slipped Chris's mind to mention it to you. Your brother really is a wimp, you know.' The scorn was not assumed, and 'wimp' was putting it mildly. Chris was an underhanded, greedy little sneak, and Clare was not an ounce better. Deed done, they had both gone about avoiding her like the plague this afternoon, not having the decency to tell her it was all over bar the shouting.

And this morning Clare had known they would be signing the sale note today when she asked Jenna to baby-sit for Jodie. Why hadn't she let on then, and at least saved her the humiliating visit to the bank manager? For a moment, Clare's betrayal piqued the most. 'I went to the bank today,' Jenna muttered in dull fury.

'So I heard,' Drew remarked drily.

And so had everybody else by now.

'Jessica will have the necessary documents drawn up by the end of next week. Your brother is very anxious for the earliest possible settlement.'

'Jessica?' Jenna pounced on the name in surprise.

'Yes, Jessica. She's very efficient—one of the best solicitors I've ever had, in fact,' Drew told her, sounding very pleased with Jessica—or himself for owning such a treasure.

'Must be very handy—having a girlfriend who happens to be a solicitor,' Jenna began shakily, and probably would have gone on to say something undeservedly nasty about the nice, friendly woman who hadn't done her any harm, but the telephone shrilled into life in the kitchen at that moment and made Jenna jump.

'Shall I?' Drew made a move towards the door.

'You don't own the place yet!' Jenna shot at him over her shoulder as she ran out of the room to silence the jarring noise before it woke Jodie.

She snatched up the receiver. 'Yes? Oh, you again, Adam.' She gave vent to her irritation before she could stop herself, and heard Drew cackle behind her.

There was a moment of huffish silence at Adam's end before he said stiffly, 'I know it's gone eleven, and I'm sorry if I alarmed you by ringing so late, but I wanted to be sure that everything was still OK with you.'

'Yes, everything is fine, darling,' Jenna all but cooed in a lightning change of voice that reduced Adam to another silence. 'It's lovely of you to ring again,' she trilled to, flaring to her roots as Drew gave another cackle. 'I'm fine,' she repeated inanely. 'And Jodie is fine. We both are.'

'We all are,' murmured Drew audibly behind her.

'I think the wind is dying down, don't you?' Jenna rattled on hurriedly raising her voice to almost a shout in case Drew tried to say anything else.

'Why are you shouting, Jenna?' asked Adam.

'I'm not shouting, Adam,' she contradicted, then gave an uncontrollable yelp as Drew's hands suddenly clasped her waist from behind and his mouth eased into the curve of her shoulder. Frantically, she tried to unpick his hands with one hand while holding the receiver in the other. When that didn't work, she tried jabbing at Drew with her elbow and making angry, growling noises of frustration that must have made Adam think she had suddenly gone barking mad.

She jammed the phone against the top of her free shoulder to cut out the sound of the tussle. 'Stop it! Stop it. What do you think you're doing?' she hissed in a furious undertone.

For a reply, Drew tightened his hands around her, and intensified the insistent gnawing at her neck.

'Oh!' Jenna cried out, and jammed the phone tightly to her ear again.

'Jenna, Jenna, are you there? What's happening?' Adam was saying urgently.

'Nothing, Adam. I . . . I thought I heard Jodie calling out,' Jenna lied breathlessly, jerking her shoulder up and down in an attempt to dislodge Drew's mouth from her neck. 'Ouch!' The cry broke out willy-nilly as his teeth gave her bare flesh a sharp little nip.

'I must go, Adam, Jodie . . .' Jenna caught her breath and arched mindlessly as the hands around her waist pushed upwards to close over her breasts. Jenna bit savagely into her lip to prevent another cry escaping. 'I must go, Adam,' she said again after an appalling moment when her eyes had closed in uncontrollable enjoyment of what Drew was doing to her.

'What about lunch tomorrow?' Adam wouldn't get off the line, and Jenna was too scared to slam the phone down in his ear.

'What? Yes, yes, fine. Goodnight, Adam.' She clattered the receiver down on to its hold at last.

Instantly, Drew released her with a laugh. Jenna spun around to him, breast heaving, face flushed with anger and the hateful, involuntary arousal. 'What do you think you were doing? That was sick!' she fumed at him. 'Disgusting!'

Drew's mouth curved with malice. 'Really? I rather thought you got quite a kick out of it.'

'You're unspeakable!'

'You didn't appear to think so a while ago back there in the sitting-room. And if you did find this last bit of lovemaking so unspeakable, why didn't you holler "rape" into the phone and have your gallant fiancé gallop over to your rescue?' he asked with a laugh, and had the satisfaction of seeing her flush even more. The last thing Jenna had wanted Adam to twig was that she had Drew Merrick in the house, let alone making love to her while she was talking on the phone!

'Was it perhaps because you knew you could not have relied on the good doctor to believe you were the blameless victim of my dastardly desires?' A set of pointed ears, and Drew would have looked a complete wolf; his grin had him half-way there.

'Oh, don't be stupid!' Jenna shot back contemptuously, before his maliciously accurate observation hit a raw nerve. Adam was a good, trusting man, but he was human too, and, Jenna had to admit, uneasy, if not actually suspicious about her reaction to seeing Drew again. Her irrational behaviour tonight would not exactly have reassured him—if he ever found out about it. Unlikely . . . but . . .

CHAPTER SEVEN

JENNA met Drew's eyes in a long, hard stare.

'As trusting as you think he is,' Drew jeered softly in an uncomfortable display of mind-reading, 'what do you think he'd say if . . .'

'Cut that out, Drew.' Jenna stopped the next predictably nasty question. 'You can make all the insinuations in the world and play your devious little games till the cows come home, but you're not going to break us up. I'm going to marry Adam.'

To spite me or yourself?' asked Drew with a sudden charge of venom. 'Adam Nash is a prig and a bore, and you'd have to be some sort of masochist to go through the engagement charade on Saturday now that you don't have to.'

'Now that you've bought me my so-called freedom, you mean? How altruistic of you,' Jenna sneered, gratingly sweet, but she couldn't keep it up for the over-whelming anger; her voice shook with it. 'Just who do you think you're trying to fool, Drew Merrick? Not me,' she told him harshly. 'I wouldn't trust you as far as I could throw you, and if you thought for one moment that your buying Chris out was going to make me change my mind about marrying Adam, you wasted your money. Insult him all you like, I'd rather marry a dozen Adam Nashes than have anything to do with someone like you. I thought I made that clear to you four years ago.'

That wiped everything off Drew's face—the last of his smugness and his tan along with it. The colour swept out of his face in front of Jenna's eyes, the sudden pallor turning the deep blue of his eyes into solid black.

'I don't believe you, Jenna,' Drew said slowly; the shakiness in his voice was new to her. Drew was hurt. It was a shock and a triumph. Her final cruel thrust had really hit home, never mind that it was a lie.

Jenna's eyes glittered. 'Don't believe what? That you haven't managed to break Adam and me up?' That wasn't what Drew meant and she knew it, but it was a safer target for her malice. 'Then come to the engagement party on Saturday and see for yourself. Why don't you?' she invited, challenged spitefully.

The stony mask was so quickly in place, Jenna might have imagined the naked hurt of a moment age. 'Thank you,' he said with freezing politenes. 'I might just do that. Now, if you'll excuse me.'

Her triumph fizzled out the instant the door closed behind him, and Jenna felt physically sick with shock at what she had said and done. The night seemed to have been one long nightmare, yet a glance at her watch told her Drew hadn't been in the house for more than an hour and a quarter—seventy-five minutes—in which she had been put through an emotional wringer from which she had come out exhausted and utterly confused. About Drew and herself.

Did Drew hate her or didn't he? Did he really believe he was doing her a favour by buying Chris out? And, if that was the case, then what did he want from her? Hardly a partnership in a business that wouldn't mean a thing to him, financially speaking. An affair? Marriage? Jenna's heart skipped a beat as the thought sprang itself on her. And if he did? Madness! What on earth was she thinking? She was committed to Adam. And she did not trust Drew. All the passion in the world, all the vulnerability to him physically, and all the traces of tenderness that nostalgia had dredged up out of the past tonight, couldn't overcome her suspicion that, one way or another, Drew meant to hurt her as much as she had hurt him.

Jenna made herself a cup of tea, and had barely finished it when Chris and Clare arrived home, and it was all she could do not to let fly at them there and then. She reined in her fury; it would keep. It was too late to start ranting now, and she was too drained anyway to take them on. Jenna muttered something about Jodie being all right and left them murmuring hasty thank yous and exchanging wary glances.

In the morning she deliberately stayed in her room until Chris left for work. It wasn't that she had changed her mind about giving him a piece of it, it was because her temper was too precarious, and she was afraid that anything she might have to say this morning would push their strained relationship to a point beyond salvaging. Somewhere at the back of her mind her brother was responsible for every awful thing that had happened to her lately. If Chris hadn't been so selfish, inconsistent, thoughtless, greedy . . . Jenna ran out of adjectives.

She heard a couple of doors slamming, followed by the start of a car engine, and then gave him a few more minutes to disappear down the drive before making her way to the kitchen. She was dressed for lunch with Adam in her best casual skirt and blouse. How she had actually managed to remember the lunch date at all was a marvel; or the work of a guilty conscience, more like, she thought miserably, and almost walked straight out of the kitchen when she found Clare and Jodie still fiddling about in there.

She exchanged a long, silent look with her sister-in-law.

'You know, don't you.' Clare wasn't asking; she was stating

Jenna said coldly, 'No thanks to you. Or Chris.'

'I'm sorry,' Clare murmured, turning a little pink and she didn't ask how Jenna had found out in between the time they had left for the dinner and returned home. Perhaps she guessed. Perhaps Drew had told them when he belatedly rejoined his party—if he did rejoin it. Or perhaps little Jodie had innocently let slip that 'Uncle Drew' had been around last night to put her back to bed. It hardly mattered how, Clare knew.

'Sorry? I should jolly well hope so! Of all the mean, cowardly things to do!' After her initial coldness, Jenna's charge of hot anger caught Clare by surprise, and Jenna too, while Jodie stopped playing with her plastic mug on the floor and crept over to Clare's side, her big eyes wide on her Aunt

Jenna.

'You might have had the decency to tell me what you were up to yesterday. Damn it, I went to see Tom Boyer at the bank, humiliating myself at the precise moment you and that coward of a brother of mine were gaily signing on the dotted line. You couldn't wait, could you? What sort of position do you think you've left me in now? Not that you care—you've got what you wanted and it's "I'm all right, Jack," isn't it?' Jenna broke off the tirade, perilously close to tears of rage. 'You couldn't wait two lousy months until Adam and I got married,' she wound up bitterly.

Her first startled alarm over, Clare's face had taken on an obstinate, pinched look—not guilt, by any means. 'I said we were sorry. And I *am* sorry if you feel put out,' she said lightly, in a considerable understatement. 'But it's everybody for themselves, and why should't we have accepted Drew's offer? A very generous offer, I might add. After all, there was no guarantee that you and Adam . . .'

It was a nasty feeling wanting to hit your pregnant sister-in-law, but that's how Jenna felt. 'Stop it! For God's sake, will you stop saying that? If I hear it one more time, I'll scream,' she threatened, just about making good the threat already.

'I only meant . . .'

'I know what you meant and you're wrong. You're all wrong, damn it, and I don't know why you keep on about it. It's driving me crazy.' And hysterical, if she wasn't careful.

Clare's face showed the sort of pained patience it

did when Jodie was having one of her rare tantrums. 'I'm sure I didn't mean to upset you, Jenna,' she said patiently—a mummy-is-not-impressed sort of voice.

'Then why in heaven's name keep on about it?' Jenna roared.

'Because . . .' Clare hesitated, then plunged in, speaking very quickly, as if to get the words out before she changed her mind. 'Because it's obvious to everyone that you don't love Adam Nash, and sometimes I think you don't even like him. I also think it was wrong of you to commit yourself to marrying Adam for our sake. Chris's sake,' she amended, 'and we were just as wrong to encourage you.' Clare was flushed and breathless, and had probably spoken more in one go than Jenna had ever heard her speak before. 'But now you don't have to marry Adam,' Clare pointed out eagerly, and looked puzzled, then angry, when Jenna pushed past the wide-eyed, silent Jodie and snatched up her handbag from the table where she had tossed it.

'You're wrong, wrong, wrong,' she muttered as she flung herself out the door.

'And everybody knows that you're still in love with Drew Merrick!' Clare got that in, triumphantly, yelling it from the doorway as Jenna ran to her car.

She always left it parked on the downward slope, and the engine rarely failed to catch by the time the car had rolled to the bottom of the drive; this time, it started on the first violent wrench of the starter, and Jenna burned down the drive at a roar, blasting fumes behind her.

It was nine-fifteen and she wasn't due to meet Adam until twelve; nearly three hours to kill. Since she couldn't go back to the house for fear of strangling Clare, Jenna drove around the island, stopping in isolated coves and staring at the sea. It didn't do much for her chaotic state of mind, but then neither would walking around the town and running the risk of having Drew materialise from around the next corner have done. Her nerves had had about as much of Drew Merrick as they could take without going to pieces.

In love with him? And everybody knew? How could they, when Jenna didn't know how she felt herself? Clare had been stabbing about in the dark—and had succeeded in making one small nick: she was right about Adam. Jenna couldn't even pretend to herself that she loved him, but she did not dislike him; Clare was wrong there. Yes, sometimes she did find Adam's stolidness and that air of self-importance irritating, but she was fond of him—very fond, Jenna corrected herself fiercely, and she meant to keep her word and marry him.

Couldn't Clare understand that she didn't want—need an 'out'? Adam loved her, wanted her, which was more than Drew did, other than for a night or two in his bed perhaps, and she would be a fool even to think of throwing away a safe, comfortable future with Adam for a fleeting affair with Drew; an affair that wouldn't be based on love, whatever Clare thought. Passion, yes, hers, Drew's perhaps, and her own deep, aching need to feel alive, and somehow more herself than Adam could make her feel.

She and Adam had never been to bed. It would not have been 'proper' until after the marriage. And that just about summed Adam up, their relationship, the island's way of life. *Proper*.

Drew had never fitted into the tight, repressive mould, and this was what had made him so exciting and different. He had broken away and made a new life for himself on his own terms. If it hadn't been for her grandmother, Jenna would have shared that life.

Ah, but for how long? she asked herself bitterly. Drew's first marriage hadn't lasted more than a year, or so island gossip had it, whereas her marriage to Adam would last a lifetime. Jenna felt a vague guilt that she couldn't find the prospect more cheering. That was just her mood; she still felt uptight and on edge as, skirting around the township, she finally headed for the small hospital complex about half a mile from the main shopping area and parked outside the gates. Adam always told her to feel free to use the hospital's parking area, as if he not only ran the hospital, but owned it. Jenna never did.

Was it her imagination, or was Adam as uptight as she was? He was waiting for her in reception, something he never did; he always came bustling along the corridor, white coat flapping, stethoscope swinging, enjoying the picture he presented of himself as the busy doctor he was. Today, though, there was no white coat, no stethoscope, no peck on the cheek either. And, but for the slight jerk of the mouth when he saw Jenna, no smile.

'Do you mind if we just have a stroll and talk first?' Adam asked as they left the main building.

Jenna threw him a sidelong glance. She was right; something was up. She said, 'No, not at all,' lightly, her nerve-ends suddenly tingling in apprehension. She searched her mind for something non-committal to start the conversational ball rolling, and found she couldn't, which made her even more uneasy, and the silence between them felt leaden. Tell him about Chris selling out, she ordered herself, but she didn't do that, either.

She hadn't realised Adam had been leading her towards the outdoor table and chairs arranged under the trees at the end of the expanse of lawn; a pleasant area where on-the-mend patients could sit in the sun or receive their visitors. Further beyond the trees was the hospital administrator's house—her and Adam's future home. Jenna made it plain that she was not prepared to live in the large Nash house under the same roof as Agnes Nash, and, a little to her surprise, Adam had conceded that point without argument.

Jenna sat down. Adam remained standing.

'Was Drew Merrick at your house when I rang you last night—the second time, I mean?' Given the question, it was remarkable Adam could have asked it and managed to sound so controlled.

Her face must have given her shock away instantly. So Adam had heard Drew laughing in the background, or heard the tussle as she had tried to free herself of him. 'Why do you ask?' Jenna countered flatly, playing for time, while her mind raced, trying to work out the best way of glossing over Drew's visit. It didn't occur to her to lie outright and say he hadn't been there. She avoided Adam's eyes.

'Was he?' Adam insisted, his voice losing a little of that repressed control, and that somehow made him less intimidating.

'Yes,' replied Jenna, woodenly.

Adam moved away from her and took a couple of edgy paces, which brought him to the other side of the table.

'Why?' Jenna asked—a stupid question when she thought about it.

Adam gave a derisive laugh. 'What sort of questions is that? It's I who wants to know "why". What was he doing there, Jenna?'

'I'd have thought your spies would have found that out for you too,' Jenna said coldly, attacking in instinctive self-defence, and amazingly it worked. A dark flush swept over Adam's face.

'I wasn't . . . I didn't . . .' Adam flustered. 'It's only that old Dr Carson went to that damned dinner of Merrick's—I'd have thought him more sensible,' he muttered in an aside, 'and he mentioned this morning that Merrick disappeared half-way through the evening, which was rather an odd, not to say rude, thing for a host to do. No one seemed to know where he'd got to, and he only returned just before people started leaving, and looking like thunder.'

'And you, or was it everybody, figured he came to see me?' It was no more than the truth, yet Jenna couldn't keep back the injured shakiness from her voice, and wondered what she was playing at. Resenting Adam's suspicions when he had every right to them? What she really couldn't get over was how accurately Adam had jumped to his conclusion. Drew was making him far more uneasy than she had realised.

'Well, he did, didn't he?' Adam growled belligerently, as if he had just remembered it wasn't he who was supposed to be on the defensive.

'Yes, he did. What of it?' Jenna shot back, and saw a sort of helplessness in Adam's eyes. It made her feel awful. 'Look, Adam,' she began, almost gently. 'Drew did come to see me, but it was only to tell me that Chris had signed the sale note that day. He was rather annoyed when he discovered during the dinner that Chris still hadn't told me; he thought I had a right to know. That's why he came.' What a preposterous lie, and how easily it had come out. Jenna felt ashamed. Yet telling him Drew had come because he knew of her phobia about storms and thought she might want company would have sounded even more preposterous than the lie.

'Funny time to do it,' Adam muttered, allowing himself to accept her lie and be mollified in spite of himself.

'I thought so, too. And told him so.' Jenna stood up.

Adam didn't move. His eyes stayed on her face. 'So now you're partners.' The tone was accusing.

'Thanks to you, yes! You see what you've done now, don't you?' Jenna turned on him in an irrational burst of blind rage, her nerves packing up on her. 'It's all your fault.'

'And just how do you come to that intriguing conclusion?' There was an uncharacteristic edge of malice in the question, a Drew Merrick type of malice and, recognising it, Jenna felt even more enraged.

'You should have told Chris on Sunday that you'd buy him out earlier than agreed, before our wedding.'

'But what if there is to be no wedding?' Adam asked, very quietly.

The question hung in the pale autumn sunshine for ages before Jenna laughed, jarringly. 'So that's it. You don't want to go through with it. I might have known Drew would get to you, make you think that he and I . . .'

Adam was shaking his head. 'Not Merrick, you, Jenna, are making me think. Do you still want to marry me?'

Her stomach seized into knots. Jenna didn't give herself a moment to think. 'Of course I do. Why shouldn't I? Nothing has changed as far as I'm concerned.' She looked at Adam very steadily.

'But things *have* changed, Jenna,' Adam contradicted tersely. 'You don't need to marry me now, do you?'

It was very hard to keep holding his eyes. 'I didn't agree to marry you just because Chris wanted to sell out and I couldn't raise the money to buy him out,' Jenna said quietly, and she honestly believed what she was saying. 'We've known each other a long time and I'm very fond of you.

'But not in love with me.'

Jenna dropped her gaze at last.

Adam sighed audibly in a sort of weary acceptance. 'The reason I didn't step in is that this way . . . well, this way you won't owe it to me to marry me.'

'Adam!' Jenna brought her eyes back to his face.

A faint, wry smile lifted the corner of Adam's mouth. 'Don't sound so shocked, my dear. You can't blame me for thinking you'd been pressed into our engagement by outside considerations. And I really thought it didn't matter to me, but perhaps it mattered more than I realised, because I'm afraid I just couldn't bring myself to step in and pre-empt Merrick's purchase. Can you understand that?' Jenna gave a small nod. 'So now, if you go through with the engagement and the wedding,' Adam continued, 'I'll know it will be because you care enough about me to want to be my wife, be part of my life and the life of this community, not out of any sort of debt to me. Only you must realise that after we're married there won't be any question of your being involved in any business venture with Drew Merrick.'

'I didn't suppose there would be. And I would hardly want it, would I?' Jenna retorted tartly.

Adam went on as if she hadn't spoken. 'You will have to sell your half before the wedding, and whether you sell to Merrick or someone else is beside the point, but sell you must.'

'I know that, Adam,' Jenna said resignedly. No chance now of hanging on to her faint thread of independence; she could read the writing on the wall.

Her docile answer cleared Adam's face of its temporary grimness. 'What about that lunch now? It'll have to be a quick one, I'm afraid.' He slipped back into his pleasant, stolid self again.

Jenna shook her head. 'I'm not very hungry, I'm sorry. Do you mind? I think I'd like to get back to the house.'

Adam didn't seem disappointed; he was relieved perhaps and Jenna felt like that, too. Even with things resolved between them, lunch would have been a strain.

The sight of workmen at the house threw Jenna into confusion. Was today Tuesday or Wednesday? Her mind did a rapid flick over the events of the past few days as she approached the young chap standing with his head thrown back, talking to his mate on the roof. It was only Tuesday, Jenna worked out as she reached him, relieved she hadn't gone potty and lost a whole day. 'Hello, you're early, aren't you? I thought you weren't due until tomorrow.'

The workman grinned. 'When Drew Merrick says "jump" our boss Mitchell says "how high?" along with everybody else on this island. Right, Terry?'

The face of Terry McPherson peered down at Jenna from the roof. 'Hi, Jenna,' he greeted her casually; they had gone to school together and Jenna liked him. 'You're top priority, didn't you know? That's what comes from being a friend, and, I hear, business associate of Mr Merrick. Lucky you.'

Terry's grin broadened.

Jenna bit back a caustic comment. 'Will the job take long?'

'Ages,' Terry said cheerfully. 'You can go and ask Mitchell—he's inside with Mr Merrick, working out what's to be done inside. All the plaster is going to have to come off, I reckon.'

'You've got to be joking!' Jenna turned on her heel and sped up the front steps to the restaurant door beside the front entrance into the house. The door was wide open, and Geoff Mitchell was standing with his back to her, bending over the reception desk with Drew leaning beside him. They both straightened up and turned to her as Jenna burst in.

Drew's eyes fixed on her coldly; he gave a curt nod of acknowledgement.

'Good afternoon, Miss Anderson,' Mitchell said politely.

'What's going on?' Jenna demanded, ignoring Drew and addressing the workman without returning his greeting.

Mitchell threw a look of uncomfortable surprise at Drew.

'Mr Mitchell has kindly consented to an early start on our premises, Jenna, and we have just finished assessing the extent of the damage which is, unfortunately, rather more considerable than first thought.' Drew answered for Mitchell, brisk and businesslike, and while Jenna had flinched at the 'our premises' she didn't dare take Drew up on it, for she was intimidated by his cold formality. His eyes met hers briefly, expressionlessly, as if she was someone he didn't know, and didn't particularly want to. It seemed unbelievable that this was the same man who had had her in his arms last night.

Jenna felt herself reddening. She addressed Mitchell again. 'How much more damage than expected?

Geoff Mitchell looked uneasy. He gave another quick glance at Drew, and when Drew said nothing, he muttered reluctantly. 'Ceiling needs replacing. And that wall.' He jerked his head at the main long wall of the room. 'Water got in at the top and the plaster has had it.'

'I'll discuss this with you shortly, Jenna. Now, if you don't mind, Mr Mitchell and I need to finish going over the quote. Please wait for me in the kitchen.' Drew turned to the papers on the desk, and Mitchell, taking his cue, did the same.

She was dismissed. Jenna marched out of the room in a fury. How dared Drew treat her like a tiresome interruption? And in front of a workman at that, as if the damage and the repairs were none of her business, or as if she was too stupid to understand what was involved.

She stormed off to the kitchen to wait for Drew; not because he had told her to, ordered, her, but because she had a few choice things to say to 'Mr' Merrick herself. She, for one, was not going to be saying 'how high?' when Drew said 'jump'.

'How dare you speak to me like that?' Jenna plunged in the moment Drew stepped in through the door from the corridor. 'How dare you put me down in front of Geoff Mitchell like that?' she demanded, eyes blazing, hands on hips.

Drew's stiffly controlled expression didn't change. 'You're over-reacting as usual, Jenna,' he said dismissively, and if he had calculated on riling her even more, he had succeeded admirably. Jenna thought she would explode. 'You interrupted us in the middle of our discussion, and I simply asked you to leave us to finish it.'

'I suppose it didn't occur to you that I had every right to be present at that discussion? It's my business too, or did that slip your mind? You don't even own your share yet,' Jenna pointed out hotly.

Drew studied her flushed face impassively. 'It was not my intention to keep anything from you, and no, I have not overlooked the fact that our partnership has yet to take effect. 'His voice was cold and clipped, a voice that must have put terror into any employee who had the misfortune to displease him. 'It was not necessary for you to be present at that point of discussion, which was why I asked you to leave.'

She was not his employee and Jenna was blowed if she was going to be intimidated. 'You mean you didn't want a silly female putting in her two-bob's worth when the big boys were discussing such important men's business as a bit of damp and replastering?' she jeered with withering scorn.

'Precisely,' Drew agreed acidly, taking her sarcasm at face value and making her feel stupid.

'And if you won't or can't be sensible about it now, then I suggest we leave this discussion until such time as we can have an adult conversation.'

CHAPTER EIGHT

JENNA wanted to tell him to go to hell, but that could wait. 'All right,' she smiled grimly, 'let's have our adult conversation. I'm selling out. To you. Now, right this minute, if you want to ring up your efficient little solicitor and have her race over with a note of sale to sign.' It was out, although prematurely. It was hardly the best way of persuading him to buy him to buy her out, but Drew forced her hand and Jenna was sick of playing along with the farcical notion of partnership.

Drew didn't bat an eyelid. 'Not interested,' he said coolly, and he threw her by his utter lack of interest, let alone surprise.

'But you must be,' Jenna heard herself protesting. 'I mean, you'd own the whole business then—the house, too. You must want that.' She persisted like a too-eager estate agent, pressuring a resisting client.

'No, thank you. A half-share suits me fine.' Drew went over to the bench and put a tentative hand against the percolator, then switched it on.

Jenna was still frowning when he turned round to her again. 'You'll have to find yourself another buyer if you're really serious about selling up. Could be difficult, what with only a half-share to offer and

131

the market being as down as it is. You might find yourself waiting six months before you get a nibble.' It was more than the truth, and Drew enjoyed bringing it home to her; the gleam of spite in his eyes told her that.

Months and months of being tied to Drew; months and months of Adam's tight-lipped resentment and disapproval. And then, of course, there would be a positive cyclone of gossip whirling around, about her and Drew. The future had never looed so awful. 'Why, Drew? Why do you want to make it so difficult for me? For us—Adam and me? How would you feel if your wife-to-be, let alone your wife, was financially involved with another man?'

'Her ex-lover?' Drew's eyebrows did a sharp jerk upwards. 'I wouldn't stand for it.' He gave a grim laugh. 'Not for a moment.'

'Exactly!' Jenna burst out triumphantly as if she had proved her point. 'Then how do you expect Adam to feel about it?'

'I couldn't care in the slightest how Dr Nash feels about it. Or about anything else,' he added airily.

'And me, Drew? Do you care at all how I feel?'

Drew shrugged for an answer. Jenna turned her face from him. What had she expected? A contrite 'Forgive me, Jenna, of course I care how you feel and I'll buy you out instantly'? After her masterstroke last night, when she had virtually confirmed Drew's belief that she had jilted him because he hadn't been good enough for her?

'How much are all the repairs and renovations going to cost?' Jenna asked abruptly, returning her eyes to him. 'And exactly how necessary are they? On Saturday I understood it was to be a matter of replacing a few tiles and fixing up a bit of ceiling. Today, it's to be a new ceiling and a new wall—new roof, for all I know. And tomorrow, What? Rebuilding the house?' The sarcasm took hold; Jenna couldn't help herself in the face of Drew's stonily impassive stare. 'Well? You wanted a business discussion and I'm ready to discuss, so how about letting me in on a few minor details?'

Infuriatingly, Drew turned his back on her and took the percolator off its stand. Jenna scowled at his back, and then at Clare, as her sister-in-law came bustling into the kitchen with a stack of clean tea-towels in her arms, looking slightly windswept but very pink and pretty, and then fatuously radiant as her eyes lighted on Drew.

'Oh, let me do that for you!' Clare dropped the towels on to the dresser and all but snatched Drew's cup out of his hand. 'You sit down, I'll pour your coffee for you,' she ordered smilingly, and Jenna could have swatted her for carrying on as if the man was incapable of pouring himself a cup of coffee.

'Lovely, thank you.' Drew smiled warmly, taking Clare's fussing as his due. But when he came to the table his eyes were hard and cold again, without a shred of warmth left in them, nor in his voice. 'Contrary to your implied accusation, Jenna, replacing the ceiling and the wall is not a whim on my part, nor on Mitchell's, to drum up some business for himself.' Drew picked up from where they were before Clare's interruption, or rather, where they would have been if he had bothered to answer her.

Jenna could almost see her sister-in-law's ears pricking up at the iciness of Drew's voice.

'The ceiling is dangerous,' Drew went on, 'and it's not a question of gluing up a few cracks and praying it doesn't come down on your customers one night, given you had any that night, of course,' he tossed in cuttingly. 'And the same goes for that exterior wall; it's rotting and needs replacing.'

'But that means the whole room will have to be repainted as well, not just one wall.'

'Obviously,' snapped Drew, and Jenna caught Clare's smirk as she brought his coffee to the table, tickled pink to hear Jenna put in her place.

'Coffee for you too, Jenna?' she offered politely, fussing about Drew, who was smiling his thanks at her.

'No, thanks,' Jenna growled, dividing a glare between them. 'That's all very well, Drew,' she recommenced heatedly, 'but we—I can't afford repaint on top of . . . '

'No, you can't, Drew cut in smoothly, 'but I can, and as a partner in this establishment I don't want to see any corners cut for the sake of a few dollars.

'A few dollars? Some people's idea of money!' Jenna glowered at the understatement.

'It's going to be done properly,' Drew continued, 'which unfortunately is going to take longer than you might wish. You'll have to remain closed for at least a month.'

'A month?'

Clare had dug out some biscuits and cheese, and put them in front of Drew.

'That's what I said.' Drew flashed another quick smile at Clare and helped himself to a biscuit. 'Not just to get the restaurant into shape again, but also to start some renovations to the rest of the house.'

'But I can't afford . . .' Jenna began to bleat the obvious again, then clamped her mouth shut in frustration.

'And while we're on the subject of finances, I'd appreciate it if you would see your solicitor about drawing up the new partnership documents in readiness for the settlement. Also, I want us to see your bank manager together some time in the near future, since I'm going to be taking over your loan when I settle with Chris.'

'No. Oh, no!' Jenna burst out in angry surprise. An enforced partnership with Drew Merrick was bad enough; owing him money was too much. Adam would have a fit! 'Can't we talk about this another time?' she muttered.

'Would you like me to leave?' Clare offered ingenuously.

'Don't be ridiculous!' Jenna snapped. 'It's your

affair as much as mine.'

'Not any more it isn't,' Clare reminded her sweetly. 'I'd better go and see what Jodie is up to.'

'What happens when the place is ready to be reopened?' Jenna had been following another train of thought and didn't like where it had led. 'I can't manage everything myself, and Clare won't be able to help for long.' Wouldn't want to, by the sound of Clare's last dig. As for Chris: wild horses wouldn't drag him near the place once he got his hands on Drew's money. Adam? Pigs might fly.

'We hire staff—chef, waitresses, anybody we need—and start running the place like the going concern it would have been if you'd given it half the chance with a bit of promotion. You'd have to be about the only person on the island sitting in an original convict-built house and hiding the fact as if it were a dirty secret.' Drew frowned as Jenna burst out with a grating laugh.

'And I suppose you'll want it renamed The Chain Gang and stage mock floggings as a floor show?' She tittered in spite of herself at the awful picture, then suddenly it wasn't funny at all. 'So where am I going to fit into your new set-up?' she asked, grimly interested.

'Wherever you like. Manageress, hostess . . .' Drew dismissed her role as if it were of no interest to him. 'Don't worry,' he reassured her drily, 'you'll be getting an income—not quite half the profits, since I'll be footing the salaries and expenses, but I dare say it'll be an improvement on what you've

been scrounging to date. Our solicitors and account-
ants can sort out the fine print later. You can
discuss the matter with your fiancé first, if you
like.'

Tell Adam she would be all but living off Drew, as
well as owing him money? Jenna smiled bitterly.
'You've got everything worked out, haven't
you?'

'I like to think so.' Drew took a final sip of his
coffee and stood up.

'Well, enjoy yourself making trouble while you
can, Drew, because you won't for long,' Jenna
hissed at him. 'I'm going to find a buyer and put a
stop to this rubbish if it's the last thing I do,' she
promised wildly on a wave of impotent anger.

'Do that,' Drew answered nonchalantly from the
door. 'But until such time as you find that needle in
the haystack, we're partners, like it or not. Please
see your solicitor at the first opportunity.'

Jenna spent Wednesday at the Nashes', the one
place on the island where there wasn't the remotest
possibility of Drew's forcing his presence on her.
The price she paid for that was hours of Agnes
Nash's repressively genteel company, attending to
the last-minute details of Saturday's party, which
was to be held at the Nashes' gracious old home. A
public place was out of the question in Agnes Nash's
genteel book, the shabby Anderson home more so.
Not that Jenna had suggested it; she loathed the very
idea of a formal engagement party. 'Betrothal' was
Mrs Nash's archaic term for it, and Jenna didn't feel

the least guilty for having left the organisation to her
future mother-in-law, who wasn't doing it for her
anyway. She was doing it for Adam, perhaps, but
mainly for her own sense of self-importance, and,
Jenna suspected, as a way of ensuring that after
such a formal and public 'bethrothal', Jenna
Anderson wouldn't dare humiliate the Nashes by
jilting their son again. It made Jenna laugh—the
irony of Agnes Nash's going all out to acquire a
daughter-in-law she didn't really want, and
certainly didn't like.

On Thursday she went out and bought a dress for
the party. She had muttered something about the
boutique getting one in especially from Sydney when
Mrs Nash had asked about it—a downright lie to
cover up the fact that Jenna hadn't been able to
bring herself even to start thinking about it yet.
Now, after a couple of frustrating hours in the
island's most fashionable boutique, she had a dress
and she felt quite unnerved at having handed over
such an amount of hard-come-by money for it.
Granted, it was a very nice dress—a simple silk in
dusky pink, which went well with her dark
colouring, its high neck and long sleeves making it
demure and sophisticated at the same time; a careful
choice which took into account her future role as
wife to Dr Adam Nash, and even Agnes Nash could
not have faulted it.

Relieved and exhausted, Jenna was treating herself to a well-deserved cup of coffee in the café
opposite the toy shop when Jessica Fenwick walked
in, and, spotting Jenna, came over to her table with

a friendly smile.

'May I join you?' she asked, and Jenna nodded, trying to keep her face from expressing how she felt at being trapped into a cosy chat with Drew Merrick's girlfriend.

'Is this your first visit to the island?' she asked, for something to say; a silly question since she knew perfectly well that it was. No one could arrive on the island unnoticed, and certainly no one as attractive as Jessica Fenwick.

'Yes. Mind you, we feel we know it like the back of our hands. Ever since we've worked for his organisation, Drew has always been mad keen to keep the island from falling into the hands of speculators, so we've been involved in his various transactions here from time to time, which has made us feel very familiar with it without actually setting foot on it,' Jessica explained lengthily, with a smile. full of lovely white teeth. She exuded such a genuine air of friendliness that, try as she might, Jenna couldn't dislike her. And why should she want to? Jessica's relationship with Drew was none of her business.

'You both work for Drew? You and Michael?' Jenna kept the conversational ball rolling out of pure curiosity.

'Yes, handy, isn't it?' replied Jessica, cryptically.

'And do you always travel with Drew—you and Michael?' Jenna hastily added. She was being nosey, and it would have served her right if Jessica had told her to mind her own business.

'Me, no. Michael usually does a lot of the travelling with Drew—being his assistant, he needs to. I run my own law firm as well as being retained by Drew, so I have my work cut out in Sydney, where I should be right now, frankly. A coffee, please.' Jessica smiled at the waitress who had come to take her order.

'Was this a sudden trip, then?' Jenna persisted with her blatant curiosity, a little surprised to find Jessica so forthcoming.

'Very. Drew had been overseas for the past six months, and he'd barely got back when the next moment we were all on our way here. We might be needed, he told us. I expect you'd notified him of the sale of your brother's share of the restaurant, and Drew wanted to get in before anyone else did,' Jessica concluded innocently.

That was one way of putting it, and Drew well might have kept Jessica in the dark about his machinations to get his hands on Chris's share—and the reason for it. Jessica seemed much too nice a person to be party to what was purely an act of revenge on Drew's part and, for a fleeting moment, Jenna was sorely tempted to enlighten her about Drew's underhand tactics.'

'Anyway,' Jessica was continuing, 'we're not sorry we came. It's been a lovely break, and we'll be really sorry to leave tomorrow. Thank you,' she murmured as the waitress brought her coffee to her, while Jenna digested the last peice of information.

'You're all leaving tomorrow, then?' The thump in her ribcage had to be relief.

'Only my husband and me. I can finish the settlement documents from Sydney, so there's no reason for us to stay on any longer, and as I said, I really need to be back at the office—Michael too, since Drew's staying on for a few days—so as not to miss your party on Saturday night. You're very old friends, I gather.'

Jenna almost choked on her coffee. Husband? No wonder Drew had smirked so smugly every time she had spoken of Jessica as his girlfriend, and Drew staying on for the party? Jenna gave a couple of strangled coughs as the coffee went down the wrong way, but this gave her time to get herself together after her shock.

'Michael is your husband?' she asked, blandly.

Faint puzzlement showed in Jessica's beautifully made-up eyes. 'Yes. I thought Drew would have mentioned it.' She frowned a little.

Not when he could enjoy himself at the expense of Jenna's ignorance. 'He may have. It probably slipped my mind,' Jenna lied quickly, letting the woman retain the crazy illusion that she and Drew had sat about for hours in pleasant chat about trivialities and old times, instead of fighting each other tooth and nail. She didn't dare ask about Drew's extended stay, because she couldn't trust herself not to give away how shocked she was by the news.

'Is this your dress for the party?' Jessica indicated the burgundy and gold carrier-bag with her eyes.

'May I see it?' she asked in a display of frank feminine interest. Jenna opened up the carrier-bag just wide enough to show the pink dress and receive an 'Oh, lovely,' on cue.

Her coffee finished, Jessica lifted her handbag from the chair beside her. 'I've enjoyed talking with you, but I really must fly now. I'm meeting Michael, ten minutes ago, to be exact,' she said with a glance at her watch and a light laugh. 'We're heading to the other side of the island to see the remains of the old convict settlement. I'm afraid we're rather left our sightseeing to the last minute, but we'll try to get in what we can.'

'Is Drew taking you?' Jenna asked, casually.

'No. He's at the hotel. Did you want to see him?' There was nothing behind Jessica's question, but Jenna felt herself flushing.

'I may drop in on him,' she admitted reluctantly, then wondered why she had wanted to keep it from Jessica; of all the people on the island, this friendly young woman was probably the only one who wouldn't think there was anything odd about Jenna Anderson visiting Drew Merrick in his hotel.

'Well, you should find him in. He had some business calls to make to Sydney this afternoon.' Jessica picked up her bill, and Jenna's as well. 'Do let me make you a present of a cup of coffee,' she smiled engagingly as Jenna was about to protest, then, standing up, put her hand out to Jenna. 'It's been a pleasure meeting you, and I wish you all the very best—and Dr Nash, too.' Her handshake was firm and warm, and Jenna found herself wishing she had got to know her a lot better.

With Jessica gone, she remained sitting there, toying with her empty cup and working herself into a stew. One moment, it seemed quite reasonable to go to see Drew in his hotel; the next, utter insanity even to think of appealing to his better nature and asking him not to come to the party. What better nature? Drew Merrick didn't have one, and if he had she would be the last person to benefit from it; his attitude at their last encounter could not have made that clearer. Jenna winced at the memory of it.

But surely Drew wouldn't have the nerve to take up her challenge and front up at the Nashs'? Oh, wouldn't he just, and he was apparently extending his stay for that very purpose. The evening would be a fiasco. Jenna had a sickening picture of Agnes Nash's frozen horror, Adam's red-faced silent fury—and herself, the centre of everybody's malicious curiosity, because Drew would see to it that he embarrassed the life out of her, one way or another. Not if she could help it! Jenna stood up with sudden decision.

Drew's hotel was the best one on the island—not surprisingly, since he owned it, having bought it some years ago when the original run-down motel had come up for sale. Jenna had never set foot in it because it was owned by Drew—not very rational of her when Drew also owned a string of shops in the town centre and she frequented those often enough, albeit out of simple necessity, since the island's best butcher operated from one of them, the newsagent from another, the coffee supplier . . .

The reception area of the hotel was spacious and comfortably furnished with easy chairs and low tables, with percolators and cups on hand on side-tables for guests to help themselves to coffee if they wanted. There were quite a number of people about. Tourists. Jenna registered the fact instantly with a surge of relief, then when she thought about it she realised it wasn't likely she was going to come across locals whiling away an afternoon in the foyer of any hotel.

But she had overlooked the staff: locals, everyone. And she had also overlooked the mechanics of getting herself to Drew's suite without knowing the layout of the hotel. There was nothing for it but to ask at reception, and her heart plummeted as she saw Dave Carter behind the counter. Chris's friend looked very dapper in his dark suit, and very surprised to see her. So much for Jenna's hope of anonymity!

'G'day, Jenna.' His professional mask slipped as he greeted her. 'Geez, I never thought I'd see the day you walked into this place. Running away from home—or come to book the honeymoon suite?' He grinned at her like a prurient schoolboy.

'Very funny, Dave. New line in PR, is it, having a bad comedian on reception?' Jenna said through her teeth, really quite angered by his cheek, and Dave had the sense to realise it.

'No offence, Jenna. Honest,' he assured her

hurriedly, dating a glance sideways to check if anyone had witnessed his breach of professionalism. 'What can I do for you?'

Jenna thought quickly on her feet. 'I'd like you to ring through to Drew Merrick's suite and ask him could he please come to reception for a moment? There's some rather important business I need to see him about.' A meeting with Drew in a busy hotel foyer was much less fodder for wagging tongues, but why did she have to explain herself to Dave? Nerves?

'Oh, yeah. I heard you and old Drew were partners or something.'

Was there anybody on the island who hadn't heard that piece of news yet? Jenna wondered wearily as Dave went to the house phone and spoke respectfully into it. It was 'Mr Merrick' this, and 'Mr Merrick' that; 'old Drew' would have been more than his job was worth, and Dave seemed to have remembered that when he came back to her. 'Mr Merrick said for you to come to his suite,' he told her, watching her face with sly interest.

'Oh, but . . .' Jenna started to say and stopped. It would look very odd now if she said she didn't need to see Drew, after all.

'D'you know where it is?'

Jenna gave a quick shake of her head.

'I'll get Tim to take you.' Dave beckoned over one of the Henderson boys, whom Jenna remembered careering around the island on his BMX all last summer and who was now almost unrecognisably spruce as the hotel bell-boy. If the island had an unemployment problem, it wasn't for want of Drew Merrick's trying to remedy it, thought Jenna as she walked beside Tim into the residential part of the building and along a wide corridor to a door marked 'Private' at the end of it.

'Thanks, Tim.' She smiled a dismissal at him, and realised that, even at Drew's door, she was still entertaining a faint hope of slipping out some back exit and bolting for it.

Tim was not to be got rid of so easily. He rapped briskly on the door and waited until Drew opened it. 'Miss Anderson, sir,' he announced in passable imitation of a butler, and only when he received a nod from Drew did he consider himself dismissed.

'Hello, Drew,' Jenna said brightly, for Tim's departing ears.

'Come in, Jenna,' Drew invited, and, if Jenna had needed any more confirmation that it had been a rotten idea to come, Drew's chilly courtesy and that equally chilling, remote look in his eyes provided it.

She stepped into the room and wished herself anywhere but where she was. 'I hope you don't mind my coming to see you,' she began nervously.

'It's always a pleasure to see you, Jenna,' Drew said urbanely, when everything else about him said it was a lie. 'Is this a business or social visit?'

Jenna didn't know how to answer. 'It's not . . . not business,' she mumbled as a compromise, and saw a light spring into Drew's eyes; they gazed into hers for an interminably long moment, looking for something, it seemed. Jenna couldn't tell whether they found it.

'I think we'll be more private in there.' Drew indicated an open doorway with a jerk of his head and, taking her eyes off his face for the first time since entering the room, Jenna saw they were in what must have been Drew's office.

The sitting-room was a normal, everyday sort of sitting-room—a far cry from the few hotel rooms Jenna had been in; paintings on the walls, a comfortable mix of old and modern furniture, and a lived-in air with newspapers and magazines lying about on the coffee-table, and an armchair. Further along, beyond the dining-alcove, a large floor-to-ceiling window gave on to the colourful lushness of the garden. A very nice home-away-from-home.

'Would you like to inspect the rest of the apartment?' Drew asked, a discernible tartness in his voice.

'Oh, no, thank you,' Jenna returned quickly, embarrassed at being caught so interested and curious.

'Then sit down, why don't you?'

Not the most gracious invitation she had heard, but why not? Jenna thought, and gave a little smile. 'Thank you,' she said, selecting the brown velvet armchair without the newspaper. 'I don't want to keep you from your business,' she added apologetically.

'You won't,' Drew told her with curt brevity.

'Would you like a glass of wine? Coffee?' There was a touch of thaw in his voice—probably because not even Drew Merrick could bark and be hospitable in the same breath.

'Nothing, thank you. I've only just had a coffee. With Jessica,' Jenna put in as a calculated afterthought, which made Drew look up sharply from pouring his drink, but only for the briefest of moments. He finished pouring the drink and closed the drink cabinet, but remained beside it, leaning against it, an elbow on the top of it. He took a sip of his gin and tonic—Jenna's favourite; she felt her mouth tingling with the vicarious taste of it, and in other circumstances would have changed her mind and had one, too.

'So, you had an enlightening chat, I suppose,' said Drew, lowering his glass. The sardonic observation didn't camouflage his curiosity; it sounded to Jenna as if he was fishing.

'Yes, very,' she agreed drily. 'Jessica told me she and her husband will be leaving the island tomorrow.' Her heart started pounding a little as she steered the conversation towards her purpose.

'That's right,' Drew nodded, keeping his eyes fixedly, on Jenna's face. 'Jessica can take care of the final details of the business settlement from the mainland, so there isn't any reason for them to stay on any longer.'

'Nor you, Drew!' Jenna shot back vehemently, leaning forward in her chair.

'Ah, you're wrong there,' Drew drawled blandly.

'I have an engagement to keep on Saturday. You can't have forgotten?' He effected mock surprise. 'It was you, after all, who issued the invitation.'

'I didn't mean it, and you know it. Please don't come, Drew.' Jenna lasped into the humiliating pleading she had hoped desperately to avoid. 'That's why I've come here now—to ask you not to come on Saturday.'

Savage little glints showed in Drew's narrowed eyes; his mouth curved in a half-quizzical smile. 'You're asking me to believe you braved the storm of island gossip just to come to rescind your invitation?' Drew shook his head slowly in a show of bemused disbelief.

'What are you talking about? Why else would I have come? And it wasn't an invitation, anyway,' Jenna told him angrily.

'All right, challlenge then,' he conceded with an unamused laugh. 'Call it what you like, I've been looking forward to taking you up on it—and any other challenge you might wish to put my way.'

There was something about the way he was look-ing at her with that unwavering, dispassionate stare that made Jenna go prickly with uneasiness. She jumped to her feet hurriedly, unable to sit there with those eyes boring into her. 'Oh, come if you want, I can't stop you,' she muttered, reaching for carrier-bag which she had put on the floor, and wanting only to get out of the room. It had been a mistake to come. Drew seemed to be implying . . . Jenna didn't quite know what but instinct told her she wouldn't like it if she did know.

Drew had his glass down on the cabinet and was across the room in a couple of swift, lithe steps. He plucked the carrier-bag out of Jenna's fingers before she realised what he was doing, and tossed it carelessly out of her reach behind the newspaper-covered armchair on the other side of the coffee-table.

'You don't want to go yet, surely,' he protested softly, in a sort of purr that sent bolts of fright through her, and which, lynx-eyed, Drew didn't miss as he stood in front of her; barring her way?

Jenna tried to suppress her alarm; they might be alone in the apartment, but there were people on call, only it was stupid to think she might actually need to call them. She was over-reacting. Or was she?

Drew's smile held dry, wry amusement—nothing sinister. Reassured, Jenna said crisply, 'I really must go, Drew, I've a lot of things to attend to,' and she made a small, tentative movement, testing whether he was really barring her way, or whether her nerves were throwing everything out of perspective.

Drew didn't move an inch, and she was locked in between him and the armchair behind her. She gave an exasperated laugh. 'Don't be silly, Drew. I want to leave, so please get out of my way.'

'Oh, no. Not yet, Jenna. Not before we've got down to the real purpose of this visit.'

Jenna's eyes widened. 'Real purpose?' she repeated. 'What real purpose? I told you, I came to ask you not to come on Saturday.'

'And you lied through your lovely white teeth, didn't you?' he laughed softly.

CHAPTER NINE

DREW'S eyes didn't have anything to do with the laugh; they sparked with a hard, bright anger, and with a threat that wasn't veiled any more.

Jenna began to shake her head. 'No,' she murmured, as if the dark blue stare had spoken its intention aloud.

'"No" what?' Drew asked softly, suddenly slipping his hands around her and locking her hard into the circle of his arms.

'What do you think you're doing? Let me go!' Jenna started struggling violently.

Drew stilled her struggle by tightening his hold. 'Come now, isn't this what you came for?'

Her heart pounding madly against his chest, Jenna shook her head dumbly.

'Oh, but I think it is,' Drew contradicted her mute denial almost teasingly, and if it hadn't been for his eyes, Jenna might have convinced herself he was only trying to annoy her by playing the fool. 'You see, Jenna, I'm afraid I don't believe for a moment that you risked your reputation, not to say your finacé's probable apoplexy, just to come to tell me to stay away from the happy occasion of your "betrothal", knowing as you must that wild horses wouldn't keep me away, invitation or no, *if* I chose to come.'

He watched her face carefully as the first appalling doubt shot into her head and lodged there. 'I don't know what you're talking about,' she flung at him angrily. 'Why else would I have come?' The heated question was to herself as much as Drew.

'Why else, indeed? Because you couldn't stay away from me, that's why—and if you weren't so riddled with those Nash-type repressions, you'd come out and admit it.'

'That's absurd,' she whispered, really shocked. 'And it's just the sort of egotistical rubbish I should have expected from you,' she rallied shakily. 'Let me go this instant!' Jenna hit out at Drew's arm, and it was like hitting a brick wall; it didn't budge. 'I'll call out, Drew. I'll scream,' she threatened wildly.

'Go ahead.' He grinned unconcernedly, knowing she would do no such thing; Jenna knew it, too.

Locked against him, she forced herself to gaze steadily into his eyes, determined not to give the slightest reaction to the arousing pressure of his body against her. 'I don't know what you think you're going to get out of this,' she said stonily.

'Not me, Jenna—you. You're the one who's hoping to get something out of it—to wit, an eleventh-hour excuse to stop yourself making the biggest mistake of your life. Isn't that right? You came here so that I would make love to you,' he went on as Jenna opened her mouth to deny his last preposterous statement. 'Afterwards, of course, you would tell yourself that in all fairness to dear, trusting Adam you had no option but to call off the farcical engagement, which I suppose would be as handy a rationalisation as any you could dredge up to avoid facing the simple, obvious truth that you're still in love with me, and that the thought of being wife to Dr Adam Nash turns you to stone.'

'That's not true!' Jenna had never heard anything more twisted than Drew's interpretation of her visit.

'Then why are you in my arms now?' he jeered smugly.

'Obviously because when brute force is applied I don't have any choice in the matter,' she retorted scathingly, and she was trying to twist out of his hold when Drew released her abruptly and took a step back—just the one step, but it was enough to leave her room to push past, snatch her bag and run for dear life.

Jenna's feet glued her to the ground. Perhaps it was the surprise at Drew's unexpected capitulation that made her slow-witted, because she just stood there, looking at him.

Drew gave a flicker of a smile. 'Well, Jenna, what now? Goodbye?'

If she walked out now, she would be walking out on the last chance to resolver the bitterness between them, the last chance to clear some of the old misunderstandings and the new doubts Drew had put into her head. She couldn't leave without trying to clear those—for her own sake, for the peace of mind Drew had taken away from her. 'Please understand, Drew, I don't need—want any excuse to break off my engagement to Adam. I told you that before,' Jenna told him again, with quiet, measured firmness. 'Whatever you think I feel for you, you're wrong. I don't . . .' She wanted to say, I don't love you any more, and found she couldn't. 'Anyway,' she rushed on, 'if I had wanted out, wouldn't I have snatched at the chance when you did your deal with Chris?' she pointed out, a little desperately.

'It's not me you need to convince,' Drew said quietly.

'Nor myself! You can hardly think I've got doubts at this stage—that I'll change my mind at the last moment!' The shake in her voice turned the statement into something that sounded suspiciously like a plea for reassurance.

'It's been known to happen before,' Drew said with tight-lipped dryness, and he wasn't referring to her first short-lived engagement to Adam.

'Maybe that's because I realised I was about to marry the wrong man,' Jenna came back at him in a surge of fierce, defensive pride.

'If you say so.' Drew let the lie pass with a faint shrug. 'Only I do want you to be sure this time.' He stepped close to her again.

Her breath quickening, Jenna stood her ground. She kept staring into Drew's face as he put a hand to her chin and lifted it up.

'No doubts, Jenna?'

About Adam—or about the tacit consent she was giving to whatever was coming next? Drew might have meant either; it was all one to Jenna. Every doubt in the world was ricocheting through her brain like a storm of hailstones as she tried to make sense of what she was doing there. She gave a sudden violent tremor. Nerves—and anticipation; and in that moment, nothing was clearer than that she wanted Drew to make love to her. No man but Drew had every made her feel this aching, breathless excitement, made her feel that nothing else mattered but to be in his arms. Just one more time and hand the consequences, the voice of unreason urged her on. She closed her eyes against the triumphant light in Drew's eyes as he lowered his mouth to her parted lips.

There was pressure in his lips, but the passion was all hers. Somewhere in the haze of desire, Jenna sensed Drew's restraint, and when he cut off the kiss with unexpected abruptness she felt cheated. 'I won't be a moment.'

He left her standing there staring after him with hurt surprise as he went into his office. Jenna couldn't believe it. Business to attend to? Now?

After a moment, Drew's voice, brisk and curt, carried back into the sitting-room. 'No calls for the rest of the afternoon. And I'm not to be disturbed under any circumstances. Is that clear?'

Oh, God, Jenna groaned in dismay as the vivid mental image of Dave Carter at reception snapping to with 'No, Mr Merrick, yes, Mr Merrick' was overtaken by an even more vivid one of Dave grinning lewdly as he put the phone down, knowing she was still in Drew's apartment; he could add two and two with prurient accuracy as easily as anyone on this island. Didn't Drew realise that, or didn't he care about her reputation?

Did she? It hardly looked like it, or she wouldn't be standing here, waiting for Drew to return. And reputation was one thing, but what had happened to her self-respect? Jenna heard the click of a key as Drew locked his office door. Nothing if not thorough; had he put a 'Do not disturb' sign out as well? This must be what people did when they were about to make love in hotel rooms: ring reception with orders not to be disturbed, go around locking themselves in. Sensible, cold-blooded preparations—enough to make anyone think twice, and Jenna did.

Another moment, and her sense of pride would have forced her to leave, but Drew came back just then, gave her a careful, unsmiling look and, putting an arm around her shoulder, steered her into his bedroom. Without a word. There wasn't any breathlessly whispered 'Come to bed, Jenna.' as he had begged the night of his dinner, and it would have been superfluous anyway, since her sole purpose for remaining was to do just that.

In the bedroom, Jenna stood frozen where he left her and watched him go to the window, which, like the one in the sitting-room, gave on to the garden, and adjust the vertical blinds carefully to let light fuse in and keep prying eyes out, taking an inordinately long time to do it, and every moment he took, Jenna urged herself to go; there was something so demeaning about standing around, patiently waiting for Drew to be ready to make love to her. Was he doing it deliberately to make her feel embarrassed? Or giving her chance after chance to come to her senses and run?

Finished with the blinds, Drew moved to the bed and looked at her steadily across it as he pulled back the covers. He did it very slowly, and so suggestively Jenna felt her face flooding with heat. Butterflies going wild in the pit of her stomach, she tried to hold his stare and failed, turning away to stare blankly at the wall.

At last he came to her, gripping hard into the tops of her arms and crushing her to him as he plunged deeply into the kiss without preamble, shocking her desire back out of its last ten minutes of numbness into fierce, instantaneous response. This was what she had been waiting for, this was what she had stood around trading her pride for, this familiar, painful sense of belonging to him, no matter how fleetingly.

She tried to wrap her arms around his neck, but Drew pushed them down to her sides, and, breaking off the kiss, held her back from himself, his eyes smouldering passion yet vaguely questioning as they combed her face.

Jenna frowned incomprehension. Could he still have doubts about her willingness? 'Oh, Drew,' she whispered urgently, 'I want to, darling. I want to so much.'

Drew made a low, growling sound deep in his throat and buried his face into the curve of her neck. Jenna held him, cradling his head to her, moaning softly into his hair and hurting with a real physical pain from the intensity of the tenderness she felt in that moment. And then Drew's hands were moving to her breast, his fingers on to the buttons of her blouse, moving down them with a fumbling haste that carried his unsureness of her, as if he were afraid that even now she was going to change her mind and rush away.

Jenna couldn't have moved if she had wanted to. She stood trembling, ice-cold with anticipation, yet her skin burning everywhere Drew touched as he undressed her. She could feel the restrained urgency in his hands—could see it in the dark, raw desire in his eyes as he stepped back from her to look at her nakedness, already possessing her in the devouring gaze that made her nipples harden and her breasts heavy and aching to be caressed.

'Please, Drew,' Jenna begged raggedly, moving to him for an end to the agonising anticipation that was racking her body with such violent spasms of trembling that she thought she would fall.

Drew was kissing her as he eased her to the bed and laid her on to it as carefully as if she had been made of porcelain, then, remaining close beside it, began to undress, watching her all the while, as dry-mouthed and mesmerised, Jenna watched him, undressing him too, every step of the way, with her eyes.

When he finally lowered himself beside her, the contact of their bodies, bare skin on bare skin, was like an electric shock. Too long suppressed, their passion flared in a blaze of white light behind her closed lids as Drew's mouth seized hers with a violence that ws almost desperate, twining his legs around her, his body bruising her, hurting. Jenna clung to him, loving and revelling in the hard, crushing strength of it.

She had never known that anything could be such torment and such bliss at the same moment. The touch of Drew's hands seared as they brushed and stroked, exploring where no man but he had ever touched before; the moist heat of his mouth worked a trail down her neck and throat and over her breats in an insistently downward path, and laid sensuous claim to every part of her as Jenna arched and tossed feverishly, crying out in wild, uncheckable whimpers while Drew brought her passion to higher and still higher peaks.

He entered her when she thought she would die if he didn't, hushing her cries with his mouth, groaning himself as his urgently thrusting body carried them both to the final dizzying peak before the tension exploded at last into a shattering release that came for Jenna in a long, satisfied cry of ecstasy drawn out from the deepest depths inside her. Drew's answering cry was a sound barely distinguishable from hers, very far away on the border of her consciousness, and only when her mind returned from wherever it had drifted away to did Jenna become aware of Drew—as Drew, as another person, and not part of herself.

Propped up on an elbow beside her, he was studying her face with an impenetrable intensity as she opened her eyes to him and smiled tremulously through a warm haze. 'I love you, Drew.' She put a hand to his cheek, tracing her fingers gently over the line of his cheekbone and down along the hard-angled outline of his jaw.

Drew continued looking at her without any change in his expression, and Jenna's hand stilled suddenly with the first dawn of apprehension. Then Drew smiled as he took her hand from his cheek and pressed the palm to his lips. 'Yes, you do,' he agreed softly, with no surprise, as if she had merely confirmed what he had known all along. Jenna waited for him to tell her he loved her too. But Drew only leant over and kissed her on the mouth, and it wasn't enough.

She freed her mouth agitatedly and gazed up at him, eyes pleading mutely. Surely he must understand how much she needed to hear those words on his lips again?

'He's never made love to you, has he?' Drew startled her with the statement—it wasn't a question—and hurt her too, that it should come at a time like this. Was it so important to him to hear her confirm that Adam had never made love to her? And was it male ego, or was it that he loved her and couldn't bear the thought of another man possessing her? Jenna couldn't tell, but the small, curious smile playing about Drew's lips told her he knew without any confirmation from her that Adam had never touched her—never more than kissed her, and even then, never broke through to the wells of passion inside her.

There had been no other man in her life; Drew had been the first, the only one, and in her heart Jenna had always known that. Now, she had to make Drew know—believe that too, had to make him understand how desperately she had regretted allowing herself to be taken in by her grandmother, how desperately she had waited for him to come back to her.

'Drew . . .' she began urgently, and was silenced by his mouth. She felt his hand slide under the sheet to her breast, and then both hand and mouth began to tease remorsely in unison, inciting her desire again, and all the apprehension, the urgent need to talk to him, was overwhelmed by the new need Drew was bent on creating in her as her body yielded to his touch.

He made love to her with an exquisite tenderness that sent honeyed warmth flowing languidly where the searing fire had burnt before. Jenna's mind and body floated as if in a dream, one in which she was calling out Drew's name over and over, and repeating, 'I love you, I love you, I love you,' like an incantation. Afterwards, fulfilled and utterly drained, she fell asleep in his arms and when she woke, Drew was gone from the bed. The disappointment was shattering.'

Jenna sat up, angry with herself for the naïvely romantic expectation she had had of waking in Drew's arms, to his warm smile, and to the 'I love you, Jenna' that she so desperately wanted to hear. The first thing her eyes fell on were her clothes folded neatly over a chair by the side of the bed, instead of lying scattered about the floor, and the thought of Drew going around picking them all up made her blush. He had left his navy terry-towelling robe for her across the end of the bed, a fresh towel thoughtfully placed beside it. Jenna slipped on the robe and went into the en-suite bathroom where the splashes of water in the shower cubicle told her she had slept right through Drew's own shower.

She showered and dressed quickly, and then stood for ages staring unseeingly through the slats of the blinds into the garden, nervous, scared, really, to go out and face Drew, not knowing what to expect any more, but feeling sick with hope that her instinct was wrong and that he wouldn't let her leave without . . . without what? At least telling her he loved her, though Jenna knew she was hoping for a lot more than that.

She found Drew sitting at the desk in his office and talking on the telephone—a perfectly reasonable activity, but one which in her uptight state of mind felt like a rebuff. So did Drew's quick, distracted smile when he looked up from making a note on the pad in front of him.

'Right. I've got that. Thanks.' Drew put the phone down, finished his jotting then stood up and came towards her. 'Would you like a drink or something to eat?' he offered pleasantly—in the way he might do to a casual guest, but surely not to the woman he had just made love so passionately.

Jenna shook her head. 'I'll have to be going,' she said, not knowing what else to say; her eyes spoke desperate volumes, begging him to put an end to her doubts and tell her he wasn't going to let her go anywhere, that he wanted her with him. Drew must have read their message, yet he ignored it.

'Right,' he said cheerfully, 'I'll walk you to your car.'

'Oh, no, thanks, don't bother. I'll be fine.' Jenna rejected his nonchalant courtesy with grotesque brightness, dying a little inside, wanting to throw herself into his arms and ask him why he was acting like this—as if nothing had happened between them when he had turned her world upside-down. Pride, what was left of it, stopped her, and pride too prevented the 'When shall I see you again?' from bursting from her lips.

He let her leave with a light kiss on the cheek, perfunctory and utterly meaningless in view of what had happened that afternoon; worse, its casualness smacked frighteningly of a casual conclusion to a casual sexual encounter. But it had not been like that. She loved Drew, and he must love her, he simply must. Yet why hadn't he said anything?

Jenna drove home bewildered, rationalising her fears away one moment and plunging back into confused despair the next. And then there was Adam. She had to tell him it was all off, again. Jenna pushed the thought out of her mind. Later, after Drew had been in touch. And he would get in touch, she promised herself on a new surge of hope. He would get in touch tonight, come over to the house, and they would tell Chris and Clare their news . . .

'Please God, let him get in touch this morning,' Jenna murmured over and over to herself all the next morning, and when the morning passed with no word from Drew, she changed the 'morning' to 'today' and prayed feverishly on, staying in the kitchen by the telephone, too scared to leave for a moment in case she missed his call. She could only be thankful that Clare had gone out early and wasn't around to see her watching the telephone like a mesmerised idiot. The workmen were about though, busy at whatever Drew had ordered them to do, and the noise of their tools and yelled conversations up and down the roof was driving Jenna demented. She couldn't think, and realised she didn't really want to. The long night of sleepless misery had exhausted every permutation of every rationalisation, and coming up with any fresh explanations for anything was beyond her.

Jenna glanced at her watch: twelve-thirty—five minutes later than the last time she had looked. Adam would be taking his lunch hour now. She must ring him and tell him she needed to see him urgently. Yes, now, Jenna ordered herself, and actually moved to the telephone and was reaching to lift it when she drew her hand back suddenly. What if Drew tried to ring and the line was engaged? She couldn't risk that; Adam would have to wait.

The sound of a car in the drive sent Jenna flying out of the side door on wings of relief, and then the disappointment of seeing Chris pulling up and Clare and Jodie climbing out of the car was like a blow to the solar plexus. She went back inside without a word.

'Hello, Jen. What have you been up to?' Chris asked carelessly, carrying a large parcel past her out into the corridor without expecting an answer.

Then Clare came in with Jodie skipping at her heels.

'Drew said to give you this,' she said, holding out Jenna's burgundy and gold carrier-bag.

Jenna stared at it, then stared at Clare. Her sister-in-law's face gave nothing away—not even curiosity—as Jenna took the bag she had left in Drew's apartment, and had not thought of until this moment.

'And he said to say goodbye for him.' Clare kept looking her steadily in the eye.

The shock of Clare's words went through Jenna very slowly, taking its time for maximum impact, and then she felt the room go into a tilt and reached to the edge of the table to steady herself.

'He left on this morning's plane,' Clare went on, her eyes, anxious now, on Jenna's white face, but otherwise giving no sign that she knew the effect of what she was telling Jenna. 'We saw him briefly at his hotel before he left. He said he'd send a manager over to take care of the renovations and run the partnership for him because he won't have any time to be involved himself any more.'

Jenna's laugh just burst out of her mouth and went on and on, wildly and out of control. She laughed until tears started streaming from her eyes and she was gasping for breath. Hysteria. And it wouldn't stop.

Clare's initial surprise had turned to consternation. She bundled a fascinated Jodie out of the kitchen and, grabbing Jenna's arm, began to shake her madly. 'Stop it, Jenna, stop it at once or I'll have to slap you. Oh, heavens!' Clare raised her hand to administer the threatening slap when, as suddenly as she had started, Jenna simply closed her mouth and stopped. And then Clare just stood there, her hand raised, looking bewildered and distressed.

'For heaven's sake, put your hand down. I'm all right,' Jenna said, brusque in her embarassment.

Clare did as she was told. 'Jenna dear, I know that . . .' she began gently, reaching for Jenna's arm—to convey sympathy or concern, or whatever else it was that Jenna didn't want.

She swatted Clare's hand away, threw the carrier-bag to the floor and made a dash out of the house, running down the back slope, scrambling, tripping over rocks, and when she got to the water's edge, she flung herself on to the sand and would have howled for the unbelievable fool she had been, but was afraid she might never stop.

She had handed Drew his revenge on a plate—and the ultimate triumph of her frantic 'I love you's' to go along with it; he must have laughed himself silly when she had gone—must still be laughing, knowing the turmoil he had left in his wake. No need for him to hang around any longer, no need to mess about with a business he didn't want just to make things difficult for her and Adam. And no need to turn up at the engagement party, spreading malice to spur the troubles along. There would be no party because Drew had seen to it that her relationship with Adam was destroyed.

Or had he?

The charge of bitter anger was the antidote Jenna needed.

* * *

The dress looked stunning.

Jenna stared dispassionately at herself in the long mirror in her room, satisfied with the image she was going to present—to Adam, to his mother, to the island. The doctor's wife-to-be looked exactly as was expected of her: elegant, understatedly sophisticated, without a hint of anything as crass as glamour about her. Or vitality.

Her face was a lifeless mask and so pale, the deeply set eyes looked large, dark holes, stary and chilly. Jenna too felt chilled to the bone, shivering every now and then, although the evening was quite mild. She wished she had a decent jacket to take with her to the party, but that would come some time in the future—mink, probably; Adam's taste was nothing if not conventional.

He had rung her several times since news of Drew's departure had spread around the island—a curiously new Adam, almost light-hearted. 'I've heard Merrick has packed up and left at last,' he had positively burbled.

'Yes, so have I.'

'Sounds like he won't be bothering with the restaurant business any more, either.' Adam hadn't been able to keep the skip-and-jump out of his voice. 'Which will make it a lot easier for you—us, I mean, darling,' he'd amended with a laugh, 'until such time as we manage to sell your half, won't it?'

'Yes,' Jenna had agreed, uninterested, and then she had gone on to agree with everything else Adam had said—about the best way to sell the business, about getting married in four weeks instead of the planned eight . . .

'No reason to put it off, is there, darling?'

'None.'

About the extra number of bottles of champagne he thought he should buy for the party, the time he wanted her to be ready to be picked up . . . She didn't resent Adam's taking over; she simply didn't care.

He was due any minute now, and she was ready as requested. Chris and Clare had already set off, Clare still looked uneasy and concerned from the events of the day before, but too scared to say a word about anything in the face of Jenna's icy remoteness since the attack of hysteria.

Jenna dabbed more colour to her lips, decided the bright slash of colour looked grotesque against the deathly white of her face, and was hastily rubbing it off when Adam's Mercedes purred up the drive. She moved to the window and watched him park, watched him getting out, impassively, as she might have watched a stranger, a blond, good-looking stranger in a beautifully cut dark suit—her future husband. To whom she would be a dutiful wife. Jenna had made that promise to herself yesterday when she had coldly, rationally, decided not to break off their relationship. And she would keep it.

She stayed watching from the window until he bounded up the steps like a happy schoolboy, waited for his 'special' knock, which oddly did not irritate her at all, then picked up her evening bag and went to open the door.

Adam's eyes lit up with admiration. 'You look

absolutely stunning,' he breathed, and made to take her into his arms.

'Darling, please, you'll crush my dress,' Jenna admonished coolly, offering an ice-cold cheek to his lips.

He kissed her dutifully, then gave her a probing look. 'Are you OK?'

'Fine, darling,' Jenna answered quickly with a brittle little laugh. 'Perhaps the start of a cold coming on. A terrible nuisance, but I'll be all right.' She put a hand on his arm. 'Shall we head off, darling? We don't want to keep the guests waiting, do we?' The 'darlings' came painlessly, and seemed perfectly natural.

Adam handed her into the car without a word and they drove all the way in silence which wasn't the least bit strained to Jenna. She stared ahead, her mind very calm . . . blank.

The Nashes' home was a blaze of light against the dark backdrop of tall pines behind it, its sandstone a warm gold under the arc lights that projected strategically on to it; the extensive garden was bathed in light too, showing off its perfection—and Agnes Nash's whip-hand over her gardners. Music and the chatter of voices wafted out of the open windows and across the wide veranda, cascading down to them as Adam pulled up beside the assembly of expensive cars in which Chris's beat-up heap stuck out like a sore thumb.

Jenna took it all in, almost in vague surprise, before the bolt of shock hit her and she flung her eyes wildly to Adam. As their eyes locked, she had the sudden sense that he knew what she was going to say; his eyes implored her not to.

'Take me home, Adam. Please,' she begged in a low, desperate whisper. 'I can't go through with it. I'm sorry.'

CHAPTER TEN

AFTER the storm, the island was cut off from the outside world for two days. The cyclone had hit in the early hours of Sunday morning, long after Adam had gone.

'All right, go to him, you deserve each other!' he had hurled at her with unforgiving anger, and kissed her in a fury of savage passion Jenna would never had believed existed in him.

Go to Drew? She had not mentioned Drew's name in her desperate, garbled explanation, but yes, she would go to Drew. Adam had jumped to the right conclusion, his reason wrong, though, because she would be going not out of love, but anger: a cold, intense anger that had crept up on her and settled in as a jagged piece of ice in her chest, and which she was afraid would dissolve into a life-long bitterness if she didn't confront its cause. Drew.

Drew might not have wanted her love—that was his prerogative—but nothing gave him the right to mock her as cruelly, cynically, as he had done, and her self-respect needed one final confrontation to tell him so.

After that, the past would truly be behind her and she could start to build a future for herself—away from the island on which she was trapped for yet another three days after power and communications had been restored, because the planes had been needed to bring in supplementary equipment and manpower, and to ferry out the tourists whose holidays had come to an abrupt end in de-roofed accommodation with makeshift facilities. Even on the Friday, when she did manage to get a seat, the plane was full of the last of the ex-holiday-makers.

Clare and Jodie saw her off, with Chris there too, typically not quite sure what anything was about, and Jenna realised with regret, and too late, how much she had underestimated her sister-in-law's kindness and generosity. Clare had been her only ally during the last awful days—the one person who believed she had done the right thing—except, iron-ically, for Agnes Nash, who told Jenna, when she went to apologise for the trouble she had caused, that she was a flighty, inconsiderate hussy, that Adam was well off without her, and the sooner she left the island the better. Jenna could not have agreed more.

'You'll be happy in Sydney, Jen, I know you will. I know things will work out for you there,' Clare had prophesied with endearing sincerity, not mentioning Drew, but Jenna read her bright, hopeful eyes and didn't have the heart to tell her Drew Merrick was very unlikely to feature in the happy new life Clare envisaged for her.

And dear, kind Clare had offered her her tiny nest-egg, enough for a week's accommodation. Having barely managed to scrape up the one-way

air fare, Jenna had accepted it with heartfelt
gratitude, as a loan, not the gift Clare wanted it to
be, determined to pay back every cent as soon as she
got a job. Any job—waitressing, sales. She was
unqualified for anything else, thanks to her grandmother's anachronistic notions that a girl need only
be brought up to be 'a lady'. And a wife. Sarah
Anderson had a lot to answer for, but the bitterness
had gone from Jenna's heart—there simply wasn't
room for it and for her anger towards Drew at the
same time.

Jenna stared impassively out of the window as the
plane landed in Sydney. Drew's adopted home
town. She didn't know where he lived, but she
would find him. When she was ready. In the
meantime, first things first. Today, a cheap hotel,
tomorrow, a job.

Loaded down with overnight bag in one hand,
handbag over her shoulder and a coat over her arm,
Jenna followed the other passengers down the
tunnelled walk-way to the waiting-lounge, all
keeping in Indian file as they came into the lounge
and walked along the roped-off section against the
wall and into the general open area. She was behind
the tall, large man who had sat in the seat in front of
her, and so she didn't see Drew right until the
moment the tall man veered sharply left, and there
she was, face to face with him.

Jenna wasn't surprised, but perhaps that was
only because there was no surprise left in her.

'What kept you?' Drew murmured with a
tentative questioning smile, possibly trying for

facetiousness which didn't come off by a long shot; his eyes were much too anxious. Jenna noted that in one flick of a freezing glance over his face before she walked past him, mechanically veering left as the tall man had done.

Drew took a surprised second or two to fall into step beside her. She sensed him, rather than saw him, because she wasn't looking at him, reaching to take the overnight bag from her. 'Don't!' she snapped, swinging the bag out of range and quickening her step.

'Jenna, I love you,' Drew said urgently. The very words she had longed for yet they didn't mean a thing. Jenna ignored them; and Drew.

'Did you hear me, Jenna? I said I love you.'

The new note of hurt impatience in his voice did it. Something went 'snap' inside her. Jenna let her overnight bag drop to the floor as she turned on him. 'Love me? Love me?' she repeated in loud, grating incredulity. 'Then you've got a damned funny way of showing it!' She really screeched at him, there, in the middle of the busy airport, startling passengers for yards around them and frightening herself out of her wits by the desperate need she had to hit him, and knowing she couldn't because somebody would probably call the police. 'Oh, go away, go away,' she mumbled, on the verge of tears of helpless frustration, stumbling to get away herself, and tripping over her bag.

Drew shot out a hand to prevent her fall, pulled her to him in the same gesture and wrapped both arms around her in a hug so tight that it hurt. 'It's all right, darling. Everything is all right now.' He soothed her like a child and Jenna stayed passive in the bear-hug for a long moment before she jerked her face out of the front of his jacket. It was not all right; far from it.

'Come on, let's get out of here.' Drew scooped up her bag, and, with the full weight of his arm crushing her shoulder, began marching her almost at a run past the gate lounges towards the escalators.

'I'm not going anywhere with you!' Jenna cried out angrily, trying to pull away from him. She felt furious with Clare, who had obviously telephoned Drew with news of her flight. Dear, kind Clare should have minded her own business. Jenna was in no state to have it out with him yet. She had not realised how much hurt was still mixed with her anger, hurt wich made her too vulnerable to any fatuous explanation Drew felt like coming up with for his cruelty.

Drew didn't bother to argue or persuade; he just kept her moving, and, short of making another scene, she had no choice but to allow herself to be jogged out of the building and across the car park to Drew's car.

'My luggage, I've got another case.' She only just remembered it as Drew was tossing her overnight bag into the back of the navy Porsche. Not that her old clothes were of any great value, but she had nothing else.

'Don't worry, I'll send someone over for it,

later,' he reassured her shortly, bundling her into the passenger seat and slamming the door on her.

'I suppose you realise there's a law against abduction,' Jenna muttered sullenly when he slid in behind the wheel.

Drew clearly thought that was funny, for he laughed. 'Why don't you have me charged? Later, though. First we're going to have to have a long talk. Not right now, when we get home, so why don't you sit back and think about all the nasty things you want to say to me?'

He was making fun of her, treating her distress as a joke, and, instead of raging at him, she had the awful feeling she might weep.

'Jenna . . .'

She stared ahead.

'Jenna, look at me, please,' Drew ordered firmly. Grudgingly, she turned her eyes to him. 'I love you. I always have. I want you to think about that too,' Drew said quietly, and started the engine.

Her mind refused to think about anything at all. She kept her eyes fixed ahead, watching, but not really seeing, the city coming into view, and the breathtaking vista of vibrant-blue harbour as Drew drove them along steep, curving roads to what seemed to be the tip of a high point of land jutting into the bay.

'Here we are,' he announced lightly, and he must have pressed a remote-control button somewhere, because the large wrought-iron gates in front of them mysteriously slid open for him to drive through.

The house was a stark, sunlit white. Later, Jenna saw it was beautiful, but she didn't even glance around as Drew led her inside and into an enormous sitting-room. She went straight to the wall of glass at the far end of the room which gave on to a patio, not because she wanted to take in the magnificent view, but because she wanted to put physical distance between herself and Drew.

The nerve-tingling awareness of him had started again during the last stretch in the car, his closeness making butterflies go mad in the pit of her stomach. If he touched her now, Jenna was afraid she would dissolve—start crying, clinging . . . forgiving; and there was a part of her that wasn't ready for reconciliation, that wanted to cut and hurt, and she needed a clear head for that, not a whirl of muddled emotion.

She took a slow, deep breath and turned from the window—almost into Drew, who had come up silently behind her. Her fright was out of all proportion. 'Don't sneak up on me like that!' Jenna shouted into his startled face. 'And you had no right to treat me as you did! No right!' she shouted in the next harsh breath, and was incensed by the blank look in Drew's eyes as he failed to make connection between the two shouts. There wasn't any connection, and he should have realised it. 'How dare you treat me like that? How dare you?'

Drew understood her this time. His mouth clamped into a thin line, and made him look angry, but his eyes showed apprehension, and he seemed unsure as to his next move now that her rage was out in the open. 'I had to do it, Jenna. There was nothing else I could do,' he said at last, very quietly—too quietly, too reasonably—a red rag to Jenna's volatile unreason.

'Had to? Nothing else you could do?' She exploded into a jeering cackle. 'You could have tried telling me that you loved me, that's what else you could have done.' Her voice quavered and cracked. 'I don't believe you do, Drew. You would never have acted the way you did if you really loved me.'

Drew threw his hands up in sheer frustration. 'Dear heaven, can't you understand? It was because I love you that I did such an awful, desperate thing to you. If I . . .'

'Aha! I knew it!' Jenna broke in with a spiteful laugh. 'Tell her you love her and she'll swallow any claptrap you want to dish out. Well, I'm not . . .'

She wasn't expecting the lunge. Drew had her roughly by both arms and was sinking his fingers viciously into the softness under the cotton sleeves of her blouse. 'Ow, let me go!' Jenna squeaked with the pain. 'That hurts. What do you think you're doing?'

'Trying to make you listen.' Drew shook her like a rag doll, sending her hair swirling into her face, then let her go with a small shove away from him.

Jenna pushed the hair out of her eyes and began to rub her arms gingerly; they felt as if a dog had sunk his teeth into them. 'Brute,' she mouthed under her breath, not daring to provoke Drew again by saying it aloud to his face.

'I meant what I said, Jenna. I do love you,' Drew said grimly through his teeth, glaring at her as if he hated her.

Still rubbing her arms, Jenna glared back in silence. 'I know my behaviour in the hotel must have seemed as inexplicable as my leaving the island without a word.' Drew paused and gave a slight shrug. 'I'm sorry about that.'

Sorry? Jenna wanted to scream at him that he hadn't just accidentally stepped on her toe; he had nearly driven her out of her mind.

'But you must understand,' Drew went on with a calm, unemotional grimness while her eyes raged at him, 'I wanted—needed you to go away and settle your relationship with Nash once and for all. Can you understand that?' he shot at her sharply, as though he were a teacher addressing an irritatingly thick pupil. 'Can you?' he repeated, and Jenna gave a hurried nod. 'I'd done everything I could to make you see that you had to end it, Jenna. I'd even forced you to admit you loved me, not him.' Drew's voice hardened. 'But I was not prepared to "rescue" you out of your committment by telling you I loved you and wanted to marry you, which was what you were waiting for me to do. You had to make the break with Nash of your own initiative, and then come to me—if you still wanted to.'

Drew may have been right, and, in spite of herself, Jenna could recognise a truth in his reasoning, but he didn't seem to have a clue how much hurt he had caused her—or didn't care, presumably figuring ends justified the means. Not for her.

'That's all very well, but it still didn't give you the right to make me feel like a tart you'd bought for an afternoon.' Jenna tried to keep the emotion out of her voice as Drew had done, and wasn't nearly so successful; it trembled and cracked all over the place. 'You couldn't have humiliated me more if you'd stuck dollar notes down my bosom on my way out. What stopped you? Couldn't you work out how much I was worth?' she jeered shakily.

Drew winced. 'Jenna, please.' He put a hand to her arm.

She gave it a quick, hard thump. 'Don't "Jenna, please" me. You were horrible and you didn't care. Oh, damn!' The tears were threatening to gush. Jenna swung away and ran along the glass wall to the french doors and on to the patio. She stood in the sunlight, dabbing at her eyes with the back of her hand. She didn't move when Drew came up beside her and put an arm around her.

'Jenna,' he said gently, 'you can't believe I enjoyed hurting you, seeing the pain in your eyes; letting you go without voicing my love, my hopes. It nearly killed me to act like a cad.'

Jenna jerked her head up at him with a harsh laugh. 'Nearly killed *you*? How do you think I felt, not knowing what to think, and then waiting all night, all morning, for you to call? The tears were stinging behind her eyelids. Jenna blinked hard.

Unexpectedly, when she needed it, Drew took his arm away and walked moodily to the edge of the patio. He turned to her, the sun at his back, his dark head glinting copper in the bright light. 'I imagine you probably felt the same as I did when I was waiting for the Cone Island plane to come in on Friday afternoon. And Saturday morning.' He smiled, bitterly, as Jenna's eyebrows shot up in uncomprehending amazement. 'And then Saturday afternoon.'

'Drew, what are you talking about?'

'The same thing you were—how it felt to wait and wait, not believing that someone you love so desperately isn't going to come. I thought, presumptuously, I know, that you'd be on the first place out to me, leaving Nash all sorted out behind you. And then I died a hundred deaths when each flight came in and you weren't on it.' Drew watched the slow dawn of comprehension over her face. He gave a little smile. 'You see, I do know how it felt. When news came of the cyclone, and the air service being messed up, I wanted to charter a plane and get over to you instantly.' He shook his head. 'I couldn't do it. I needed you to come to me, and kept going to that wretched airport and waiting. I had to keep hoping I was right, and that you loved me enough and that it wouldn't be like the last time.'

Jenna stared in horror. The last time? Had Drew waited for her like that four years ago, too? The heart-tearing picture in her mind made her feel weak. She ran to him, wrapping her arms around him, just holding him to her. 'Oh, Drew, you can't imagine . . . if only you knew how much I wanted to come. I never stopped loving you, never stopped hoping you would come back for me. I wanted to die when I heard you got married.' She lifted her face up to look into his eyes. 'Why did you?' she asked despairingly, and felt his shoulder lift under her arm.

'I suppose because I convinced myself that the old girl had really got to you and you'd changed your mind about me. You can't blame me,' he added defensively.

Jenna hadn't meant to sound accusing, and she didn't blame him for anything any more; she just needed to know. 'What was she like?' She flushed a little for the curiosity she couldn't suppress about the woman who had been Drew's wife.

Drew contemplated her with a faint frown. Gauging how much to tell her? Had the woman been so awful? Jenna wondered, and realised she was hoping she had been, because the thought of Drew loving somebody else, even for a short time, was unbearable.

'Very nice. She was a very nice girl,' Drew

smiled, and put paid to Jenna's irrational
assumption that he would say 'a right bitch' and
that she had been the first woman he had picked up
on his way back from the airport when he finally
realised Jenna wasn't going to come.

'Oh,' Jenna said woodenly, wishing she hadn't
asked.

Drew lifted a hand to her hair and entwined his
fingers into her curls. 'She was tall and slim,' he
began, with a soft reminiscence in his voice that
made Jenna go rigid with jealousy. 'Like you. And
she was dark-haired like you, and sometimes even
looked a little like you.' Drew's fingers stopped
playing in her hair. 'But she wasn't you, and it was
rotten of me to marry her for the illusion,' he
finished gruffly.

'Then why didn't you come back after your
divorce?' Jenna asked after a moment of trying not
to feel delighted that the woman had never
possessed his heart; she was too female not to be
pleased. 'I would have left Gran, I'd seen through
her and . . .'

'And if she'd actually died of rage, you would
never have forgiven yourself—nor me,' Drew cut in
with his own end to her sentence. 'And if she hadn't
died we'd have had her anger between us. You
would have been miserable, I realised that, and
resigned myself to waiting. I have to confess I
followed the death notices like a ghoul.' Drew
grinned sheepishly. 'But then, as fate would have it,
I was abroad when she did die, and when I got back
and heard you were married, I thought I'd blown it

for good.'

'Married? But I . . .'

'No, of course, you weren't. My investment advisor had his facts wrong for once, thank God. He'd heard you and Chris had opened a restaurant but wanted to sell it because you had just married the local doctor. Can you imagine how I felt when I heard that?' Jenna could feel Drew's shudder against her. 'Fortunately, I've never been one to take anyone's word without checking, and so I found out you had only become engaged, unofficially, at that, and I was on the first plane over to put a spanner in the works any way I could—with all the subtlety of a sledge-hammer, I admit, but there simply wasn't time for finesse with all the odds against me. You seemed so convinced you hated me, or I hated you—both, probably. I also had to face the unpalatable possibility that you might have actually had second thoughts about him and really fallen for that prig, Nash.

'That's not fair!' Jenna pulled back from the warm circle of Drew's arms. 'Adam is a good man and I won't hear you speak of him like that, Drew. I mean it,' Jenna said crossly.

'Truce, I take it back,' he laughed.

Jenna wasn't amused. 'What I did to Adam was unspeakable—and I did it twice. He won't ever forgive me, and I don't blame him.' It seemed so unfair to have gained so much happiness for herself at the cost of anybody's hurt.

'Don't brood on it, darling,' Drew said gently his amusement gone. 'Believe me, Dr Nash will soon find some nice, conventional girl who'll think he's wonderful and be content with the life of no surprises that he'll provide for her.' Drew was leading her across the patio and back into the house. 'That girl could never have been you, Jenna. You couldn't have take the sort of life Adam or the island could offer. You never belonged there, any more I did. We're two of a kind; we might love the place, but there's no room for us to breathe there, to be ourselves. We need wider spaces.'

Clare had tried to express something similar when Jenna had told her she was leaving the island. Jenna felt a surge of affection for her perceptive sister-in-law . . . perceptive on a lot of counts.

'What are we going to do about the restaurant?' she asked suddenly, the thought of Clare reminding her of it

'Whatever you like,' Drew answered, steering her through the large sitting-room with a very definite destination obviously in mind.

'I don't think I ever want to go near it again,' Jenna told him firmly. She didn't want to go near the island either, for a long, long time.

'Right. I'll put it on the market—both our shares. Someone local will want it. It's a very good time to sell.'

Jenna pulled them up short at the bedroom door. 'What? You told me it was a rotten time to sell, you liar,' she chided with mock severity.

'All's fair in love and war, haven't you heard?'

Drew smiled lingeringly into her eyes as he bent to kiss her. 'Our war is over, my darling, and it's time for love,' he murmured into her lips.

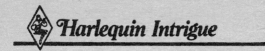

Harlequin Intrigue

Two exciting new stories each month.

Each title mixes a contemporary, sophisticated romance with the surprising twists and turns of a puzzler...romance with "something more."

Because romance can be quite an adventure.

Intrg-1

Romance, Suspense and Adventure

Harlequin Romance

Coming Next Month

#2965 NO GREATER JOY Rosemary Carter
Alison fights hard against her attraction to Clint, driven by
bitter memories of a past betrayal. However, handsome,
confident, wealthy Clint Demaine isn't a man to take no for
an answer.

#2966 A BUSINESS ARRANGEMENT Kate Denton
When Lauren advertises for a husband interested in a businesslike approach to marriage, she doesn't expect a proposal from a
handsome Dallas attorney. If only love were part of the
bargain....

#2967 THE LATIMORE BRIDE Emma Goldrick
Mattie Latimore expects problems—supervising a lengthy
engineering project in the Sudan is going to be a daunting
experience. Yet heat, desert and hostile African tribes are
nothing compared to the challenge of Ryan Quinn. (More about
the Latimore family introduced in THE ROAD and TEMPERED
BY FIRE.)

#2968 MODEL FOR LOVE Rosemary Hammond
Felicia doesn't want to get involved with handsome financial
wizard Adam St. John—he reminds her of the man who once
broke her heart. So she's leery of asking him to let her sculpt
him—it might just be playing with fire!

#2969 CENTREFOLD Valerie Parv
Helping her twin sister out of a tight spot seems no big deal to
Danni—until she learns she's supposed to deceive
Rowan Traynor, her sister's boyfriend. When he discovers the
switch his reaction is a complete surprise to Danni....

#2970 THAT DEAR PERFECTION Alison York
A half share in a Welsh perfume factory is a far cry from Sophie's
usual job as a model, but she looks on it as an exciting
challenge. It is unfortunate that Ben Ross, her new partner,
looks on Sophie as a gold digger.

Available in March wherever paperback books are sold, or
through Harlequin Reader Service:

In the U.S.
901 Fuhrmann Blvd.
P.O. Box 1397
Buffalo, N.Y. 14240-1397

In Canada
P.O. Box 603
Fort Erie, Ontario
L2A 5X3

ATTRACTIVE, SPACE SAVING BOOK RACK

Display your most prized novels on this handsome and sturdy book rack. The hand-rubbed walnut finish will blend into your library decor with quiet elegance, providing a practical organizer for your favorite hard-or soft-covered books.

Only $9.95

Approximately 16" x 8" when assembled

Assembles in seconds!

To order, rush your name, address and zip code, along with a check or money order for $10.70* ($9.95 plus 75¢ postage and handling) payable to *Harlequin Reader Service*:

Harlequin Reader Service
Book Rack Offer
901 Fuhrmann Blvd.
P.O. Box 1396
Buffalo, NY 14269-1396

Offer not available in Canada.

BKR-1A

*New York and Iowa residents add appropriate sales tax.

Keepsake